ON THIN ICE

"What do you think we should work on?" Nikki asked, skating over to Alex.

"That death spiral."

"Do you think so?" Nikki felt a wave of doubt. The move still scared her, especially when her head skimmed the ice as Alex spinned her around.

Alex nodded. "Why not?" He pulled off his sweatshirt and tossed it into the bleachers.

Think positive, Nikki told herself as Alex took her hand. Stay relaxed, she repeated again and again as they skated around the rink, trying to build up speed and power.

Finally they were ready to go into the spiral. As Alex spun her faster and faster, Nikki lay back until she was almost parallel to the ice. But her body was tense, and she felt her skating foot begin to wobble. At that moment Alex let go of her. . . .

Silver Blades

titles in Large-Print Editions:

THE
PERFECT PAIR

＞～　～＜

Melissa Lowell

Created by Parachute Press

Gareth Stevens Publishing
MILWAUKEE

For a free color catalog describing Gareth Stevens' list of high-quality books and multimedia programs, call 1-800-542-2595 (USA) or 1-800-461-9120 (Canada). Gareth Stevens Publishing's Fax: (414) 225-0377. See our catalog, too, on the World Wide Web: http://gsinc.com

Library of Congress Cataloging-in-Publication Data

Lowell, Melissa.
    The perfect pair / Melissa Lowell.
      p.   cm. — (Silver blades; #5)
      Summary: Nikki and her ice skating partner Alex have some rough times when their relationship off the ice starts to get confused with their skating.
      ISBN 0-8368-2067-3 (lib. bdg.)
      [1. Ice skating—Fiction. 2. Friendship—Fiction.]
      I. Title. II. Series: Lowell, Melissa. Silver blades; #5.
      PZ7.L96456Pg   1998
      [Fic]—dc21   97-39605

First published in this edition in 1998 by
Gareth Stevens Publishing
1555 North RiverCenter Drive, Suite 201
Milwaukee, WI 53212 USA

Printed in the United States of America

1 2 3 4 5 6 7 8 9 02 01 00 99 98

'I wish Jill still lived here," Nikki Simon declared. It was a sunny May day in downtown Seneca Hills, Pennsylvania, and Nikki and her two best friends, Danielle Panati and Tori Carsen, were shopping at the Spring Sidewalk Sale for a present for their friend Jill Wong.

The three thirteen-year-old girls all belonged to a skating club called Silver Blades, and Jill had been a member, too, until several months ago, when she'd moved to Colorado to begin training at a well-known skating academy.

The stores along Main Street were all displaying their goods for the annual outdoor sale. Danielle admired a brightly colored sports watch. "This would look great on Jill, wouldn't it, Nikki?"

But Nikki wasn't listening. "If Jill were here, we

could have a big party to celebrate," she said wistfully. She tossed back her long brown braid and slipped her sunglasses down over her green eyes.

"If Jill hadn't moved to Colorado, we wouldn't have anything to celebrate," Danielle reminded her as they moved on to the table outside Retro Rosy's secondhand boutique.

"You're right, Dani," said Tori. "If Jill had stayed in Seneca Hills, she certainly wouldn't have placed third in the Rocky Mountain Spring Skate Fest last weekend. She wouldn't have *skated* in the competition at all."

"And she wouldn't have been on cable TV!" Danielle added.

"Or needed a surprise present from the three of us." Nikki laughed. "All right. I get the point. If Jill were still in Silver Blades, we wouldn't be celebrating anything."

Nikki had a warm laugh and a big smile, even though she was self-conscious about showing off too much of her braces. She was slender and had high cheekbones and a slightly turned-out walk, like a dancer. And today she was even dressed like a dancer, with a long, filmy earth-toned print skirt over a black unitard and black leather ankle boots.

For as long as she could remember, Nikki had dreamed of being a gold-medal Olympic figure skater. Her family had moved to Seneca Hills from Missouri last fall so that Nikki could try out for Silver Blades. It was one of the top skating clubs in the country. She had aced her audition and started training as a pairs skater with her partner, Alex Beekman, a few months ago.

"The trouble with Jill's training so far away at the International Ice Academy is we aren't a foursome anymore," Danielle remarked.

"I know what you mean," Nikki said. "Whenever we hang out together now, I feel sort of like a car with three wheels."

Tori was eyeing the racks of retro clothes critically. Her mother was a clothing designer, and Tori considered herself the group's fashion expert.

"Actually I've been spending a lot of time lately with Haley Arthur. She moved across town to my block a few months ago," Tori said. "She's really fun. You know Haley, don't you?"

Danielle laughed. "Of course we do. She *is* Nikki's main competition."

"Right," Nikki said with a sigh. *Competition.* Nikki was getting tired of the word. She wished there were some way to become a great figure skater without always having to compete against people she knew. Twelve-year-old Haley was part of Silver Blades' number-one pairs team. Haley and her partner, Michael Bass, had won the gold medal in the North Atlantic Regional Competition last January in Lake Placid. Nikki and Alex didn't compete, although they'd gone to the competition to cheer their friends on. It would be a few more months yet before they, too, were good enough to skate in front of judges.

"Haley goes to Kent, too," Tori continued. "Even though she's only in sixth grade, she's *very* cool. She really wants to be friends with you guys too."

Kent Academy was a local private school that Tori, Alex, and several other Silver Blades skaters attended. Nikki and Danielle went to the public school, Grandview Middle School.

"Let's all go for pizza sometime," Tori suggested.

Nikki managed a small smile. "Sure, sometime," she said, trying to sound neutral. She had nothing *against* Haley Arthur. But she was surprised that Tori liked her so much. After all, Haley was a year younger than they were, and she was a tomboy—not very much like Tori, who cared a lot about how she looked. Tori had long curly blond hair and huge blue eyes and always wore the most fashionable clothes.

Nikki looked up and down Main Street, hoping one of the displays would inspire her. She wanted Jill's present to be silly, easy to mail, and inexpensive. All at once Nikki grinned. She made a beeline for a table outside a toy store, Kid City.

"Hey, guys, look at this," Nikki called to her friends. "*Here's* something Jill would flip over!"

"It *is* red—and red is Jill's favorite color." Danielle sounded doubtful as she fingered the fuzzy red stuffed animal. "But I still think we should get something she can wear to the rink at the Ice Academy so that she'll remember the good old days here at Silver Blades."

Tori rolled her eyes and groaned. "Really, Dani, the last thing Jill needs is another red headband for her hair or a pair of red leg warmers. And Nikki, you've got to be kidding! This is beyond dumb. I don't even know what kind of animal it's supposed to be!" She put the toy back on the table with a thump.

Before Nikki could protest, another voice chirped in.

"That looks like an ostrich that got run over by a truck. *I* think it's great. Stuffed roadkill!"

Nikki turned around and found herself face-to-face with a redheaded girl wearing baggy black shorts, a purple T-shirt, and black combat boots. She wore a black baseball cap sideways and had a small silver-dagger earring in only one ear.

"Haley!" Tori cried, smiling. "You *would* love something so dorky." Tori then looked past Haley. "You're still hanging out with your usual gang. Don't you have any friends who aren't boys?"

Nikki followed Tori's gaze. Sure enough, in front of the sporting goods store were four guys. Nikki knew two of them—her partner and Haley's. Michael was lacing up a new pair of in-line skates while Alex leaned against a display of baseball caps, talking to a blond high school girl.

As usual Alex looked more confident and casual than any other fourteen-year-old boy Nikki knew. He was wearing a pair of ripped-up jeans and a brown leather jacket that made his eyes and curly hair look darker. Nikki couldn't quite figure out why he looked older than the other guys he was with. Was he just a little taller, with slightly broader shoulders? Or was it the way he looked so comfortable talking to a pretty girl? Nikki wasn't sure what it was, but Alex definitely seemed older—a lot older—than her own boyfriend, Kyle Dorset.

"So who's the ugly red stuffed animal for?" Haley asked.

"I thought it would be a good present for Jill Wong," Nikki replied, a little offended.

"She'd like it. It's red," Haley said. "I heard she placed third in the Skate Fest."

Nikki nodded. "Yeah, isn't it great? We're *so* happy for her! That's why we thought we'd chip in and send her something. But Dani and Tori don't like—"

"Well, if *Haley* thinks it's cool . . ." Tori interrupted, giving the red plush animal another look. "Let's do it. Let's get this. Okay, Dani?"

Danielle's mouth dropped open. Nikki couldn't quite believe her ears. Tori rarely listened to *anyone* when it came to questions of style.

"Sure, Tori," Danielle agreed.

"And I'll mail it. Mom will let me use her Express Mail account," Tori volunteered, pulling a couple of dollars out of her wallet and handing them to Nikki.

"Thanks," Nikki said, still a little surprised, but really glad Tori had changed her mind. The funny-looking stuffed animal was just the sort of thing goofy Jill would love. Nikki was sure of it.

"I'll contribute too," Haley offered with a smile. She dug her fist into her pocket.

"I didn't know you knew Jill." Nikki smiled politely,

but inside she felt annoyed. Why was Haley trying to butt in on something she wasn't part of?

"I guess everyone at Silver Blades knows Jill and misses her," Tori said.

Haley gave Tori a friendly punch. "Oh, come on, Tori. You can't tell me you aren't just a teeny bit glad she left, even if she was one of your best friends. Now you don't have to try to outjump her in front of the judges anymore—at least not until the Nationals."

Tori looked a little hurt. "That's not fair, Haley. I miss her as much as anyone."

"I was only kidding," Haley said quickly.

"So this is where all the skaters hang out!" Alex declared as he approached the girls. "Why didn't somebody tell me?" Nikki liked Alex's great dimples and the way his dark eyes sparkled when he smiled. She knew very well why all the girls at the rink were jealous that she got to skate with him.

Alex shoved his hands in the pockets of his baggy jeans and winked at Nikki. "So you do exist outside the rink," he teased.

"Yeah." Nikki gave him a quick smile. "I don't see you much outside of practice either."

Nikki was never quite sure how to act with Alex when they weren't skating. Sometimes she wished there was a handbook called "How to Behave with Your Pairs Partner Off the Ice." Boys, except for Kyle, made her feel a little nervous and unsure of herself. And Alex seemed sure of everything.

"We *should* hang out together once in a while," Alex said easily. Nikki felt herself blush a little, and wasn't quite sure why.

Just then Michael Bass skated up to join them. Haley's partner was muscular, with dark blond wavy hair and a face that was usually smiling. He never seemed to be able to sit still. Nikki thought he was cute but not as handsome as Alex. He paused to slap Haley a high-five.

"How about heading over to Ken's Arcade?" Michael asked. "The guys really want to go." He gestured and pointed to the two other guys who were standing behind him. "They've got a hot new Captain Laser and the Zodiac Crew Caper there."

"I haven't tried it yet," Haley said. "Let's go over there until it's time to get to the rink."

"I'm psyched," said Alex. "You girls want to come?"

Tori shook her head firmly. "No way. *We*'re having a girls' day out, and you guys aren't invited."

"We are?" Danielle asked, looking disappointed. "They aren't?"

"Definitely," Nikki quickly chimed in. She wouldn't feel comfortable around four guys, two of whom she didn't know at all, hanging out at an arcade.

"And Mr. Arndt from Seneca Sportswear sent me a card saying they're having a sale on skates. I want to buy a pair," Tori announced. She looked at Haley. "And since Haley's one of the girls, she'll come with us."

"I will?" Haley looked uncertainly from Nikki and

Danielle and Tori to Alex. After a moment she grinned. "Why not? It'll be fun to hang out with the girls for a change."

Alex shrugged. "Whatever . . ." He turned to Nikki. "See you later at the rink." He started off, then turned around again. "Hey, maybe we could hang out at the mall sometime. I'll call you. Maybe we could go some Friday night."

"Okay." Nikki wrinkled her nose as she watched the boys head off. Hanging out with Alex would be fun, but it seemed a little odd that he had asked her. Was he asking her on a date? Did he know she had a boyfriend?

"Alex is a hunk," Danielle said as the four girls headed into Seneca Sportswear. "What's he really like?"

"He's great to skate with," Nikki replied as she paused in front of the skate display. She ran her finger appreciatively down the new leather on a boot, and checked out the price. "Alex is a fantastic skater, and I love being his partner."

Danielle groaned. "I *know* that. But what's he like, *off* the ice?"

As Nikki sat down on a bench in the shoe department, she realized she knew very little about Alex's personal life. At the rink they only talked skating. "I know that he lives just with his father. His mother died when he was a little kid. But I really don't know much more about him," Nikki admitted.

"That's weird," Haley said. "I know everything about

Michael." She screwed up her face and giggled. "More than I want to. We're good friends, though."

"I guess Alex and I aren't really friends," Nikki said. "Even though I spend a lot of time with him."

Just then the salesgirl walked up, and the girls gave her their sizes. A moment later they were all opening boxes of skates.

"Alex has lots of friends," Tori chimed in. "And a lot of them are girls."

"Girlfriends?" Nikki asked curiously as she put the skate back in the box.

"I don't know," Tori admitted. "I think he dates. I don't see much of him around Kent, since he's in eighth grade. I can't imagine him not dating, though. He's pretty comfortable around girls."

Nikki pulled off her ankle boots and picked up her right skate again. She closed her eyes, savoring the smell of the new leather. Why did new skates always feel so good?

She slipped her foot in and wriggled her toes. Something was stuck in the boot. Probably tissue paper, she thought. And then, through the thin fabric of her tights, her toe touched something cold and squishy.

"Oooooooooh!" she shrieked.

Nikki quickly kicked off the skate. It flew across the aisle and landed on the floor.

"A spider!" Tori and Danielle screamed, as a big black spider popped out of the boot and landed inches from Nikki's foot.

"Oooooh!" Nikki screeched again. She jumped on top of the bench and clutched her long skirt tight against her legs.

Spiders terrified Nikki. She hated them. Just looking at one made her stomach lurch. Covering her eyes with her hands, Nikki cried, "Get rid of that thing!"

"It's humongous," Tori declared. "I'm not touching it."

Danielle squinted at the black blob. Then she leaned down to take a closer look. "It's just a *rubber* spider." She picked up the spider between her thumb and index finger. With a devilish grin she jiggled it in front of Tori's nose.

Nikki forced herself to peek between her fingers. Hesitantly she stared at the spider in Danielle's hand. "Rubber?" she repeated. The spider looked awfully real to her.

Haley began laughing so hard, she was doubled over.

"Is something wrong?" the store manager, Mr. Arndt, asked as he hurried toward them from the stockroom. He was a heavy man with a round, red face.

"No," Danielle said quickly as she hid the fake spider behind her back. "Just a little joke, Mr. Arndt."

"Sorry we made so much noise, Mr. Arndt." Tori flashed the flustered manager her sweetest smile. Mr. Arndt's eyes were now glued to Nikki.

Suddenly Nikki felt very silly cowering on the bench. With a sheepish smile she eased herself onto the seat. She noticed that Haley, hanging back by a rack of sweatshirts, was still laughing.

"How did that thing get in my skate?" Nikki finally demanded after Mr. Arndt had returned to the stockroom.

Haley broke into a new round of giggles.

Tori took the spider from Danielle and threw it at Haley. "You turkey!" she said to Haley, but she couldn't keep a straight face. Then she was laughing as hard as Haley.

Nikki pressed her lips together and took a deep breath. "Haley, you put that spider in my skate?"

"Yeah!" Haley was still smiling. But she shifted from foot to foot. "Hey, you look pretty freaked—"

"Don't you ever, *ever* do that again!" Nikki jumped off the bench and stood very straight. She was very embarrassed, and her heart was thumping double-time. "What were you trying to prove?"

The laugh froze on Haley's lips. She looked genu-inely confused. "Uh—nothing. I didn't think you'd get so upset. It was just a joke." She touched Nikki's arm. "I'm sorry."

Nikki pulled away.

Tori rushed to Haley's defense. "Lighten up, Nikki. Haley always plays jokes like this." Tori put her new skates back in their box and handed them to the sales-girl, along with her mother's credit card. While she waited for her receipt, she poked Haley playfully. "Tell Nikki and Dani about when you first met Michael, Haley."

Haley grinned. "I don't know—it was nothing real-ly."

Tori picked up the story. "Haley skated right up to Michael at the rink. Their old coach, Jon Linder, was standing there with Kathy Bart, who was also coaching. Michael went to shake Haley's hand, and she gave him one of those bloody rubber hands with shredded fingers to shake. It really grossed him out."

"In front of Kathy Bart?" Danielle's brown eyes went wide. "You did that?" She sounded very impressed.

Haley chuckled. "You should have seen Kathy's face! You *know* how 'The Sarge' hates us to horse around on the ice—especially during lesson time." Haley deepened her voice, knit her brow, and waggled a finger under Tori's nose. " 'Skating's serious business.' "

Haley sounded just like Kathy. Nikki felt a small smile tug at her lips.

Tori grinned. "C'mon, Nikki. Picture it. Michael about to circle the rink with a bloody fake hand."

Nikki's smile widened. "Yeah, it *is* a funny picture." She hated to admit it, but Haley was pretty funny sometimes. "You sure know how to make friends, Haley," she commented.

"Nikki!" Kyle Dorset called over the country music that was blaring out of the loudspeakers of Seneca Hills Ice Arena. His shout broke Nikki's concentration.

Nikki was on the ice warming up by herself until Alex arrived. Haley and Michael were finishing up their coaching session with Kathy Bart. It was late afternoon, and only a few members of the skating club were still practicing. Alex and Nikki were scheduled for the last coaching session of the day.

Kyle called out again. Nikki turned to wave at him, noticing that his broad shoulders looked even broader in his hockey practice gear. Even from across the Olympic-size rink Nikki could see he was really excited about something.

A small shower of ice flew up beside Nikki as she came to a stop only inches from Kyle. She pulled a tissue out of her sleeve and blew her nose. As usual the rink was cold and had turned the tip of her nose red. Nikki leaned against the barrier rail and returned his shy smile.

"We did it!" he announced. He ran a hand through his longish brown hair. It was damp with sweat, and his cheeks were still pink from exertion. Kyle was the center forward on the Seneca Hills Hawks. The local hockey team played and practiced in the second rink in the arena. "We won the game against the Watertown Tigers."

"All right!" Nikki cheered.

She waited for Kyle to say more. Instead he rocked back and forth on his skates and just grinned. As usual he wasn't about to brag, but he'd probably played a big part in his team's victory.

"Did you score any goals?" Nikki asked him. Out of the corner of her eye she spotted Alex taking the ice. Hilary Ford and Kelly O'Reilly, two eight-year-old girls in Silver Blades, were draped over the barrier, watching him as they giggled and sipped hot chocolate.

Kyle's grin widened. "Yeah. Two out of four goals," he told Nikki. "I guess I sort of won the game for us."

"*Sort of?*" Nikki felt so proud. "That's really, really great, Kyle."

Before she could say more, a hand squeezed her shoulder. "Ready to hit the ice?" Alex's voice was deeper than Kyle's. Nikki looked up at him. "Nice sweatshirt," he said. Nikki tugged down the new yellow sweatshirt she was wearing over her black tights and leotard. She blushed a little.

"Uh—thanks," she said. "I got it today."

"It's great," Alex said. He gestured toward their coach, who was shouting out instructions to Haley over a Garth Brooks ballad. "We'd better start warming up. Kathy's almost done torturing the gruesome twosome for today."

Nikki laughed. "Stop calling them that, Alex. You know you like Michael."

"And Haley. Still they *are* the competition." He wriggled his eyebrows, and Nikki laughed again.

Kyle cleared his throat.

Nikki had almost forgotten about him. "I'll be right there," she told Alex, and pushed him away gently. He pretended to lose his balance as he glided backward across the ice.

Nikki smiled apologetically at Kyle. "I do have to warm up now," she said. "I'm really glad to hear about the game."

"Yeah!" Kyle kicked his skate against the rubber matting that covered the floor leading away from the rink. His smile looked a little forced. "I guess I'll call you later," he said after another pause.

"Okay," Nikki replied.

Suddenly a cheer went up from the little girls watching from the sidelines. Alex was going into the preparation for a double axel. Nikki watched as he landed the difficult jump perfectly.

"All right," she murmured.

"I think hockey's more fun for a guy," Kyle said suddenly.

"I think you're jealous," Nikki teased. She batted him with the end of her ponytail. "You probably can't do that!"

Kyle's smile collapsed.

Instantly she wished she'd kept her mouth shut. "Not to worry!" she said quickly. She rested her hand lightly on his arm. "Alex couldn't score two goals in a hockey game."

Kyle nodded. "Right. Probably doesn't know one end of a hockey stick from the other."

"Can't tell a puck from a Ping-Pong ball!" Nikki joked.

By now Kyle was grinning again. "Talk to you later," he said as he left the rink.

"Right," Nikki called after him, then skated away from the barrier with a smile on her face. She *really* liked Kyle, but he was incredibly shy. Nikki had met him right after moving to Seneca Hills last fall. Somehow, even with all their figure-skating and ice-hockey practice, they managed to see each other a couple of times a week. But Nikki still found it hard to talk to Kyle. He wasn't at all like Alex, who never had trouble talking or joking about anything . . . with anyone! Nikki sighed. In some ways it was easier to be with Alex than Kyle, even though she hardly knew Alex personally at all.

"How can Haley and Michael *stand* that country music?" Alex asked when Nikki skated up. They joined hands. His were warm and dry and sure, and Nikki, as usual, felt safe and secure on the ice with him. Hands still linked, they skated in perfect unison around one end of the rink, carefully avoiding Haley and Michael. Kathy was drilling them on a new lift-and-throw combination.

For a moment Nikki and Alex watched the other pairs team. No matter what Alex said, the upbeat country tune suited the pair perfectly—particularly Haley. She had a great sense of rhythm and a quirky, comical style. Her footwork was incredibly quick and neat, and she was one of the most agile skaters Nikki had ever seen. Now she was practicing a series of Arabian cartwheels, which resembled no-handed cartwheels. Haley landed each one perfectly on the ice, then sprang up into her partner's arms.

Alex whistled under his breath. "She's sure got nerve!"

"Haley's pretty fearless," Nikki said, feeling envious. She knew that Haley had trained in gymnastics before she fell in love with skating. Nothing Kathy Bart cooked up for Michael and Haley seemed to faze Haley. Nikki was pretty brave on the ice herself, but she was no match for Haley when it came to gymnastic stunts.

Alex seemed to sense her mood. "But we're better than they are!" He leaned down and confided, "She's nervy, but you're a more beautiful skater."

Nikki was flattered, and a little flustered too. She'd never received such a personal compliment from a boy before. To cover up, she laughed and said, "Thanks, but face it, those two have already won a gold. Haley's a year younger than I am, and Kathy doesn't even think we're good enough to compete yet."

"Not true," Alex contradicted. "We just need a little more experience together." He paused to peel off his red sweatshirt. Underneath he had a gray long-sleeved T-shirt over black stretchy pants. Alex tossed his sweatshirt into the stands, then took Nikki's hands. Together they skated backward. "We can do anything," he said, picking up speed.

As Nikki glided along with Alex, she found his confidence contagious. "You know, Alex, I think you could be right," she said, and she really meant it. Since they'd started working out together several months ago, they had made tremendous progress. In the beginning Nikki had had to get used to not skating alone, but by now it was second nature. In fact, now it would feel weird to skate alone.

"You bet I'm right," Alex said with a toss of his head. "Once we get our chance in front of the judges, Haley and Michael are history."

Before Nikki could respond, Kathy skated up. Her dark-blond ponytail bounced against her navy-blue sweater. She grinned at the pair over the rim of her coffee cup. "So, you guys ready for work?" she asked.

Nikki and Alex nodded.

"Today let's run through the second half of your freestyle program. I've already advanced your tape."

Alex and Nikki positioned themselves at opposite ends of the rink from each other. As the opening strains of *Swan Lake* started, Nikki counted the first four beats. Then, with strong, solid strokes, she skated backward across the rink toward Alex. She went into a preparation for a star lift. Alex's left hand closed tightly on hers, and his right hand was on her waist. With a powerful spring, Nikki jumped into Alex's arms, then was suddenly high above his head.

"Let go of her left hand!" Kathy yelled to Alex. "And Nikki, hold your position. Don't let that back leg flop."

"Here goes . . ." Nikki heard Alex say. "Let's see if all that work in the weight room paid off."

Nikki caught her breath as Alex let go of her hand and held her just by the waist. For the first time ever, Alex was supporting Nikki with one hand. As he held her, Nikki felt as if she were flying. She was so far above the ground, and she felt weightless. It was a great feeling—truly exhilarating. She landed effortlessly on the ice and skated smoothly into a wonderful combination of dance steps that she loved. It all happened so naturally, so perfectly, that Nikki automatically broke into a wide smile.

"Great!" Kathy shouted, and Nikki flushed at the rare compliment from their demanding coach.

"Made for each other!" Kathy yelled.

From the squeeze of Alex's hand Nikki knew Alex thought so too.

3

'**M**ade for each other!' I heard Kathy say that. 'Made for each other!' " Haley chanted as Nikki entered the locker room a few minutes later.

"The Sarge said *that*?" Tori looked awed. "I'm impressed."

"Way to go, Nikki!" Haley exclaimed, plopping on her baseball cap.

Nikki looked up from unlacing her skates and said, "I owe a lot to Alex, that's for sure. He's a real pro."

"He sure is," Haley agreed, "and so are you!" Nikki smiled shyly at Haley, grateful for her support. Haley grinned back and said, "You two are perfect partners."

"Oooh, sounds romantic. Like true love," Tori remarked.

Danielle giggled.

"True love? No way!" Haley crinkled her nose in disgust.

"Pairs partners have been known to fall in love!" Tori remarked a little smugly. "The great Russian pairs team that won the Olympic gold medal in 1964 and 1968, the Protopopovs, fell in love and got married."

True love? With Alex? The thought had never crossed Nikki's mind before. She loved *skating* with Alex, but she had never thought of him as a possible boyfriend. What would it be like to date him? she wondered. Would we have enough to talk about? Would we become really close? She pulled her skates off and listened carefully to Haley debating Tori. Haley *did* have more experience at pairs.

Haley shook her head violently. "Ugh. Love. Forget it." She tied her combat boot, then planted her hands on her hips. "The perfect partner has to be the right height for you and skate in the same style as you do. But really he's someone that sort of fits you like the perfect skating boot—except you don't have to break him in."

"It's like chemistry," Tori suggested.

"Still sounds romantic to me," Danielle muttered.

"The first time Alex and I skated together, it *was* easier than I thought it would be," Nikki mused.

Haley snapped her fingers. "Exactly! And it shows. Michael and I are pretty good together. We have the same sort of style, and our timing's good, and we're real pals"—Haley looked thoughtful—"but he's not what I would call my perfect partner."

"You did win a gold at the Novice Regionals last month," Tori reminded Haley. "And I heard Kathy and Mr. Weiler say you guys are heavy favorites for the Novice Nationals next winter. How much more perfect can you get?"

Haley laughed. "Yeah. I know what you mean. But my ideal skater would be more into gymnastics and definitely more of a ham. Michael's sort of shy."

"Would your perfect partner have red hair, too?" Tori teased.

Haley laughed again. "Then we'd match!" she joked. "But seriously, a lot of things go into finding the perfect partner."

Just then Danielle checked her watch and whistled. "Hey, guys," she said to Tori and Nikki. "I don't know about you, but I'm starving. Mom's picking us up any minute now. She said you can all come to Giovanni's with us for pizza." She glanced at Haley. "You can come too," she added politely. Nikki knew Danielle was trying to be nice by including Haley, but she didn't sound overly enthusiastic.

Haley didn't seem to notice. She beamed. "Oh, I'd love to! But I can't! Can I take a rain check?" Haley sounded a little proud as she announced, "Tori's coming over to my place for a sleepover."

"A sleepover?" Danielle echoed.

"You are?" Nikki asked Tori.

Tori shouldered her skate bag and heaved a dramatic sigh. "Mom's on a business trip till Monday. It was either that or get a baby-sitter." Tori made a sour face. "Can you believe it? I'm thirteen years old and my mother still won't let me stay alone when she's out of town. Haley came to my rescue."

"My parents already made a reservation for dinner somewhere, otherwise I'd ask you guys to come along," Haley explained.

"We're going to be late," Tori said, and headed for the door. "Talk to you guys soon."

Haley waved good-bye and trotted after Tori. The locker-room door slammed shut behind them.

"A sleepover?" Danielle and Nikki cried in unison.

"They're tighter than I thought," Danielle said, swinging her feet back and forth as she sat on the bench. "Haley's okay, but she's a weird match for Tori."

"Really. Tori's so into clothes and makeup and stuff. Haley's such a tomboy." Nikki shook her head. "Maybe Tori's just hanging out with her because they go to school together."

"Yeah, but Tori and I have been good friends so long," Danielle said, sounding sad. "Now she's spending all her time with Haley. I know she wants us to start hanging out with Haley, too, but I don't know. . . ."

Nikki fingered the silver-skate charm she wore around her neck. She felt a little out-of-sync with Haley, too, fun as she was. And Nikki missed Jill.

Tori, Jill, and Danielle had given Nikki the charm when she qualified for Silver Blades. They all wore one too. It was a sign of their special friendship. "I just feel if Jill were here, we'd all be heading out together after practice. Especially since it's Saturday," she said.

"I guess it's just us tonight," Danielle said to Nikki. "But later I'm going to write Jill a real 'wish you were here' letter describing every bite of Giovanni's pizza."

"Don't mention the present," Nikki warned. "Tori will mail it Monday. Let Jill be really surprised." Nikki began to brush her hair and chuckled. "It's probably better Haley doesn't come with us for pizza anyway," she added. "Who knows what she's got stashed in her skate bag. Cheese-colored rubber worms?"

Danielle grinned. "I'd love to serve that up to Nicholas."

"I wouldn't start playing jokes like that on your brother. He's obnoxious enough as it is," Nikki said.

"Dani, are you in there?" Danielle's mother's voice drifted through the locker-room door.

"Out in a minute, Mom. Nikki's still getting changed," Danielle called.

"Be ready in a second!" Nikki shouted as she put her skirt back on. "I think I could inhale half a Giovanni's super deluxe all by myself."

Later that evening Nikki bounded up the four steps leading to the front porch of the old Tudor house where her family lived. At the top of the steps Nikki turned around and waved at the Panatis' Volvo.

Nikki pushed open the front door and practically floated into the hall. "I'm home!" she announced. She peeked in the living room. The television was off and the study door was closed. She was about to start up the stairs leading to her room, but quickly skidded to a halt.

She sniffed. Weird, she thought. No yummy food smells coming from the kitchen. The Simon kitchen always smelled wonderful, even hours after dinner was prepared. Her mother was a great cook and had been thinking of opening a gourmet-catering business. Had her parents eaten out too?

"Mom?" she called.

"She's upstairs," her dad answered from the dining room.

Nikki walked down the hall and poked her head into the dining room. The round oak table was heaped with the old shoe boxes where her father kept all the bills and household records. He peered at her over his glasses. "Hi, Niks." He flashed her a smile, then glanced down at his paperwork. He had moved his computer in from the study. The screen cast a pale light on his face.

"You guys ate already?" Nikki asked.

Mr. Simon looked up again. He was a slightly heavy man, with Nikki's green eyes and freckles. "I had a sandwich. No time for dinner tonight."

That's strange, Nikki thought. The Simons never had sandwiches for dinner. And something else seemed weird. "You're working tonight, Dad? It's Saturday."

"Just figuring out our finances," he said. His fingers danced over the calculator keys.

"Are we having money problems?" she asked, concerned. She knew her skating lessons were very expensive. Though her father had a good job, her parents also had to make a lot of sacrifices for her skating.

Her dad looked up quickly. "No," he said, his face softening into a smile. "Things couldn't be better. Just playing with the budget. Nothing for you to worry about." He blew her a kiss and went back to jotting figures down on a yellow pad.

"Oh." Nikki was relieved . . . sort of. She stood waiting for him to say something else. It was the first time since she moved to Seneca Hills he hadn't asked her about her skating lesson. And tonight she was eager to tell him about the star lift she and Alex had done.

But to Nikki her dad looked as if his mind were orbiting some other planet. Before she could ask him what was going on, the phone rang. Her mother called from upstairs. "It's for you, Nikki. It's Kyle."

Nikki dashed up the stairs and ran down the hall to her room. Tossing her skate bag on the bed, she picked up the phone. "I've got it, Mom," she called, and waited until she heard the receiver on the extension click.

"Hi," she said, cradling the yellow phone on her shoulder. She flopped down on the bed, kicked off her shoes, and propped a pillow under her head.

"So what's new?" Kyle asked.

"We did it!" she said. "Alex and I did a real star lift!"

"Sounds great, but what is it?"

Nikki explained. As she talked, she twirled the yellow phone cord around like a jump rope. She felt breathless and happy and forgot all about her father and the bills and the cluttered dining room table downstairs.

"So you sort of scored goals today too!" Kyle sounded proud of her.

Nikki laughed and agreed.

There was a pause, then Kyle cleared his throat. "I called because I wondered . . . you know . . . if next Saturday afternoon . . ." He cleared his throat again. "If you would like to go to a soccer game at the high school after practice and your lesson with Kathy."

"Sure," she said. But before she could say more, the phone clicked. It was call waiting. "Oops, we've got another call. Hold on," she said.

She pressed the receiver. "Hello?"

"Hi, Nikki!" a voice said over the phone.

"Alex?"

"Your one and only partner," he announced cheerfully.

"I'm on the other line, can you hold a minute?" she asked, wondering why he was calling her.

She clicked the receiver again. "Kyle?"

"Yeah."

"Can you hold a minute? It's Alex."

Kyle didn't answer for a second. "Oh, well—yeah— I guess."

"Great, I'll be right back." Nikki clicked off Kyle and asked Alex what was up.

"I told you I'd call."

"That's right, you did," Nikki said, remembering that today at the sidewalk sale he had said he'd call sometime.

"Anyway," Alex went on, before she could tell him that she couldn't talk just then. "I've got some really great news. You're not going to believe this." He sounded very upbeat.

"What?" Nikki glanced at the blue plastic clock on her wall. It was sandwiched between a poster of Kristi Yamaguchi doing a lovely layback spin and a ballet poster from *Swan Lake*. She didn't want to keep Kyle waiting too long.

"You know my dad is a theater-set designer."

Nikki nodded. "Yes." Tori had told her that Mr. Beekman was a very famous set designer and that they were very wealthy. Alex and his dad lived in one of the fancy new condos that overlooked the golf course of the Kent Country Club.

"Well, he got hold of some tickets for the American Ballet Theater's *Romeo and Juliet* next Saturday—the matinee."

Nikki wasn't quite sure why he was telling her this. "So?"

"So?" Alex laughed, and mimicked her voice. "So, do you want to go with me? They're great seats and—"

"Go to see *Romeo and Juliet*? The ballet?" Nikki exclaimed.

"Yes." Alex paused. "I mean if you aren't busy."

"Busy?" Nikki started laughing. She'd never be too busy to go to a ballet. Acres of hot coals, herds of wild horses—nothing could keep her from going. She adored ballet. Sometimes she thought if she couldn't be a skater, she'd be a ballet dancer. Ballet lessons were her favorite part of the off-ice training at Silver Blades, and she always tried to use the ballet steps she learned in her skating programs.

She let her head sink into the heap of pillows on her bed. She'd seen lots of ballets on video and on TV, but she'd only been to a live ballet performance once, back in Missouri. It wasn't a very good company, just a local amateur group. She could believe she'd get to see the American Ballet Theater perform one of her all-time favorite ballets, live, in person! Wait till I tell Tori, she thought.

"But I can't—we can't," she realized abruptly, feeling hugely disappointed. "We've got that special session lined up with Kathy. She wants to put our whole free-style program together with all the music next week. She said she needed all Saturday afternoon and—"

"No sweat." Alex sounded smug. "I checked it out with the Sarge after practice. She said the ballet would be perfect for us. Sort of like a field trip. She said we'd get some pointers just by watching the dancers."

Nikki couldn't believe it. Kathy Bart was a total fanatic about never missing coaching sessions. "She did?"

"No lie. She practically ordered us to go. And there's

a chance my dad can pull some strings and maybe we can get backstage and meet some dancers. He knows everyone in the biz," Alex said.

"We can go backstage?" Nikki whooped with joy.

"Then it's a date?" Alex asked.

"I have to ask my mom. Hold on a minute." Nikki tossed the phone on the bed. "Hey, Mom," she shouted, running into the hall.

"In here," her mother called from the spare bedroom.

Nikki practically flew into the small room. "Mom, Alex is on the phone, and Kathy says it's . . ." Her voice trailed off.

Her mother looked up. "Hi, hon." She smiled. Her smile was broad and warm like Nikki's, but she looked a little pale.

Nikki stared at her mother, then at the room. It was smaller than Nikki's, and her parents hadn't changed the pink flowered wallpaper since they moved in last fall. Two large trunks were open, and her mother seemed to be clearing everything out of the tall oak dresser. The contents of the closet was already piled around the room.

"What's going on?" It looked as if they were going to move again.

"Spring cleaning," her mother said after a moment's hesitation. She avoided meeting Nikki's eyes, and Nikki knew something was wrong. Mrs. Simon loved to cook and hated doing housework, especially stuff like spring cleaning.

Nikki wanted to ask her more questions, but there wasn't time. "Look, Mom, Alex wants me to go to the ballet with him next Saturday and—"

"Sure, as long as you have a way of getting there," Mrs. Simon said, and went back to folding up a pile of old flannel nightgowns.

"Great," Nikki said, and hurried back to the phone. "Alex, she said yes."

"Knew she would," Alex said.

Nikki had been sure her mother would, too, but she was a little surprised that her mom hadn't asked first about her lesson or about getting permission from Kathy or anything like that.

Nikki shrugged, then flopped back down on the bed. She dreamily walked her feet up the wall as she and Alex made plans for next Saturday.

Suddenly Nikki heard the grandfather clock in the downstairs hall chime eleven. "Oh no!" she cried. "Alex, we've got to hang up. I've got a singles makeup lesson with Kathy at six tomorrow morning." Nikki still took singles lessons twice a week, even though she really loved pairs skating.

"But it's Sunday." The ice arena was open to the public all day Sunday, and the rinks were too crowded for either hockey practice or skating lessons.

"I know, but Kathy arranged to come in before the place gets crowded. I gotta go."

"Right. See you Monday," Alex said. "And remember, next Saturday."

"How could I forget!" Nikki said.

"Then it's a date!" Alex said.

As she hung up the phone, Nikki's face hurt from smiling so much. This was one field trip she was really going to love. She couldn't wait to tell the other kids at the rink. Danielle didn't like ballet much, but Tori would absolutely die. And . . .

"KYLE!" she suddenly exclaimed. She had forgotten all about Kyle!

She grabbed the phone and pressed the receiver. Nothing. No call waiting. No Kyle. Just a dial tone. She had left him on hold that whole time.

"Oh, no. What do I do now?" Nikki cried. She glanced up at her clock. It was too late to call him.

Then she remembered the soccer game next Saturday and groaned. "I don't believe this," she muttered. "How did I get into this mess? Kyle is going to be so angry. What am I going to tell him?"

She sat down hard on the edge of her bed, cradling her head in her hands. Somehow, some way, she had to figure out how to tell Kyle she hadn't meant to forget he was on hold. But even worse, how was she going to break her date with him for Saturday?

4

"**H**as anyone seen Kyle today?" Nikki asked Tori, Danielle, and Haley. It was Monday afternoon, and they had just finished their weight-training session.

"No," the three girls chorused as they entered the snack bar. They all wanted a cold drink before they got on the ice.

The noise level was high. The radio music was blaring, and the round Formica tables were full of skaters. But the one person Nikki was looking for wasn't there.

Kyle seemed to have vanished from Seneca Hills. When Nikki had called his house Sunday, no one was home. And she felt too shy to talk to his family's answering machine.

Today in school she hadn't run into Kyle either. Nikki had a queasy feeling that he was trying to avoid her.

"Be right back," Nikki said suddenly as she spotted Kyle. He was with Jordan McShane, who was Danielle's boyfriend, and Nicholas Panati, Danielle's brother. The three of them were approaching the snack bar before hockey practice. She felt shy talking to him in front of the other guys, but she couldn't miss her chance to explain everything. "Kyle," she called across the snack bar.

He looked up. She waved. He did not look happy to see her. Nikki blew out her breath and forced herself to march up to him. Luckily Jordan and Nicholas went to talk to some other hockey players.

"I've been trying to find you all day," Nikki said, not quite able to meet Kyle's eyes.

"Why?" Kyle demanded, sounding hurt.

This was *not* going to be easy, but Nikki went on. "I'm sorry about the other night when I left you on hold." Saying it sounded so stupid. She rubbed one foot on top of the other and stared down at her shoes. Say something, she silently urged him.

"Right"—Kyle paused—"to talk to Alex."

This time Nikki did look at him. His blue eyes looked hurt. He was jealous. *Of Alex?* "Yeah, but—" she started to explain.

Someone yanked her ponytail. "Ouch," she cried, and turned around. She found herself face-to-face with Alex. "Alex," she said sharply. "Don't do that!" She hadn't meant to overreact, but she couldn't help herself. Alex was about to make an awkward situation even worse.

Alex backed off, holding his hands up in front of him. "Hey, don't be so touchy." He thumped his broad chest. "It's only me. Your one and only partner." Then he noticed Kyle. "Hey, Dorset. What's up?"

"I wouldn't know," Kyle said, then gave Nikki a look. "See ya later."

"Kyle," she called after him. "I've got to talk to you." But he didn't bother to turn around. Nikki's shoulders slumped and she sighed.

"What's with him?" Alex asked. They left the snack bar and headed for the rink.

"Nothing," Nikki told him. "But sometimes, Alex, your timing's rotten."

Alex faked a pained expression. "What? I'm your partner. Our timing has to be perfect."

As they headed for the ice, Haley jogged up, saying, "Hey, wait up, you two." Nikki and Alex stopped outside the door to the rink.

"I was watching you the other day, after Michael and I finished our lesson," Haley said as she removed the rubber guards on her skates and stepped onto the ice. "You both looked great," Haley continued. "But I noticed you were having a little trouble with that death spiral."

Nikki nodded. The death spiral was the one pairs move that really scared Nikki. It was a hard move, one that meant she had to trust Alex completely. He had to hold on to her while she lay back with her head only inches from the surface of the ice, and he spun her around.

"Kathy hasn't said much about it." Alex sounded a little defensive.

"She's concentrating on your lifts," Haley said. "But a really good death spiral will blow away the judges."

"So what exactly was wrong?" Nikki asked. Off the ice she wasn't sure she could trust Haley not to play some dumb joke. But when it came to skating, she knew Haley wouldn't joke around. Suddenly Nikki was glad that Tori had made her and Haley become friends. Nikki liked the idea of knowing another girl in the club who could share the special problems of skating pairs.

"Your body position is wrong," Haley answered. "It's as if you're afraid to let go."

"I am," Nikki admitted. "I'm afraid Alex will drop me on my head." She glanced at Alex, hoping he wasn't offended.

"I've dropped you before," Alex reminded her. "From some pretty high lifts."

"That's different. I don't even think about falling on my head with a throw or a lift," Nikki said.

"I can show you what you're doing wrong," Haley offered.

"Sure," said Nikki.

Haley took Alex's hand. They skated around the rink a couple of times, getting the feel of each other. Then Haley talked Alex through a couple of combinations. Nikki recognized them from Haley's program with Michael. As they went into the death spiral, Alex began pivoting. He held Haley tightly and spun her around by one arm. She was lying back almost horizontal to the surface of the ice. "This is how *you* do it, Nikki," Haley shouted.

Nikki could see how stiff and awkward Haley looked, like a diving board or plank of wood. That's how I hold myself? she wondered.

"If you fell like this, you probably *would* get really hurt," Haley said, coming out of the spin. "You're all tight and tense. Now I'll show you the right way." This time, when Alex spun her around, Haley's whole body seemed lighter, and her head was back and almost grazing the surface of the ice. Suddenly she let go of Alex's hand. Nikki gasped. But Haley managed to fall right on her rear and skidded, laughing, across the ice. When she came to a stop, she sat up and said, "And that's how you fall, without getting hurt doing it."

"Let's give it a try," Alex said, sounding eager.

Nikki was eager too. Sure enough, with the image of Haley's death spiral in her head, Nikki felt better about the move. Haley's instructions had been really clear and helpful, and the younger girl's form was terrific. Nikki and Alex practiced a few times, with Haley shouting encouragement.

"Wow!" Alex said to Nikki after their fifth try. "You picked that right up." He grabbed his towel and draped it around his neck. Bending over from the waist, he tried to catch his breath.

"I think I've got it," Nikki agreed. She felt a rush of excitement, and her heart was beating rapidly.

"Thanks, Haley," she added warmly. She skated back and forth in front of Haley as she cooled down. "Hey, you're going to make a great coach someday," Nikki said.

"What me—coach? Like the Sarge?" Haley faked a horrified expression, then her face softened into a goofy smile. "But," Haley added, skating alongside Nikki, "I *do* like teaching and helping people. And I don't get much of a chance yet. So thanks."

"I mean it," Nikki added warmly.

She heard Kathy talking to Mr. Weiler, the other Silver Blades coach, over by the rink's door. Any minute now Nikki and Alex's lesson was due to start. She couldn't wait to see if Kathy would notice that she and Alex had improved their death spiral. Nikki hooked her leg over the railing of the barrier and stretched, bending her nose to her knee.

"Umm, I was wondering," Haley hesitated.

Nikki looked up.

"Could we go to the mall together sometime?"

"Shopping?" Nikki asked.

"And without Tori . . ." Haley looked a little embarrassed. "I need to put together a new skating outfit. Tori's always trying to dress me up too much. She's got great taste, but it's too frilly for me, especially for our new country routine."

Nikki straightened up and returned Haley's smile. "There's a new Western-wear store opening up next to Sundaes in a week or two," she said, feeling flattered.

"Buckaroos!" Haley said. "I saw the sign. Maybe we can put something together from there."

"Great minds think alike," Nikki said as Kathy came onto the ice. "I can't wait to check the store out. It'll really be fun," she added, and she meant it. She waved good-bye to Haley. As Alex took her hand to begin their program, Nikki decided that Haley Arthur wasn't so bad after all.

5

"Nikki!" Danielle clutched Nikki's sleeve as the two girls walked into the crowded front hall of Grandview Middle School the next morning. "Look at your locker!" she cried.

Nikki gasped. "Balloons?" She couldn't quite believe her eyes. A huge bouquet of balloons in the Silver Blades colors—white, blue, and silver—hovered above her locker, near the ceiling.

"Who in the world would do that?" Nikki wondered aloud.

"I'll give you three guesses!" Danielle chuckled. "Beginning with Kyle Dorset—he's probably sorry about what happened yesterday at the ice arena snack bar."

Nikki began to smile as Danielle steered her through the crowd of sixth-, seventh-, and eighth-graders who were streaming toward their homerooms. "It must have been Kyle," Nikki agreed happily.

Jordan McShane was stuffing his Seneca Hawks jacket into his locker as the girls walked up. He greeted Nikki with a big grin. "Yo, Nikki!" he said. "Win some contest or something?"

Nikki shook her head and blushed a little at all the attention. Everyone seemed to be staring at her. She fingered the ribbons and lopsided bow that tied the balloons to her locker. Kyle must have brought the balloons in early, right after morning hockey practice. Nikki felt a silly smile spread across her face. She hadn't even had a chance to explain about Alex to him, and he had sent her a present.

"So who's your fan?" asked Nicholas. Danielle's older brother tugged Nikki's ponytail. Nicholas and Jordan's lockers were across from Danielle and Nikki's. Nicholas looked a lot like Danielle, but with short, spiky brown hair. Jordan had dark, wavy hair and a dimple in his chin.

Danielle groaned. "Get outta here, Nicholas." She shoved her brother aside. "Oh, Nikki. There's a note. How romantic!"

"What's romantic about sticking a note to a locker with masking tape?" Nicholas commented.

"Isn't that *special?*" Jordan added in a teasing tone.

Danielle faked looking hurt, until Jordan mugged a goofy face. He launched into an imitation of Donald Duck's voice. "See ya later," he quacked, and gave her a quick hug. Danielle rolled her eyes as he headed for his eighth-grade homeroom.

"What is wrong with this picture?" Danielle said. "The guy I like is an escapee from Toontown, and your boyfriend sends you great presents."

Nikki still couldn't believe it. Kyle was usually too shy to do something this showy. And he never seemed to have much money.

Kara Logan and a group of her friends crowded around. Kara was a seventh-grader like Nikki, and she lived next door to the Simons. Kara was one of the coolest kids in school. Nikki liked her a lot, even though Nikki was usually too busy with skating to spend much time with anyone besides her Silver Blades friends.

Nikki handed Danielle her book bag and carefully removed the small white envelope stuck to her locker.

"What did Kyle say?" Danielle was as excited as Nikki.

"Come on, Nikki," Kara urged, tugging Nikki's sleeve. "Open it."

The first warning bell rang, and Kara sighed. "I can't be late again, I'll get detention. But catch me up on this later. Maybe I'll have a real scoop for the school paper's gossip column."

Nikki waited until Kara and her friends were safely around the corner before she opened the card.

"What's it say?" Danielle bounced a little on her toes.

Nikki's green eyes grew very wide. "It's not from Kyle."

Danielle draped her arm on Nikki's shoulder and

read the note aloud. " 'For my perfect partner . . . ' It's from ALEX!" Danielle looked very impressed. "That's really cool. He's even sending you presents now."

Nikki felt happy but confused. "I wonder why he sent them," she said.

"Because he likes you," Danielle stated.

Nikki shook her head. "I don't think so. He's just happy we had a great session yesterday." Nikki hurriedly explained about the death spiral and how impressed Kathy had been with them as she pulled more books from her locker, then stuffed her jacket in the bottom. She struggled to close it tight enough to lock. The second warning bell rang just as she hooked her combination lock through the handle.

"Now I'm going to be late, and what do I do with these balloons?" she asked Danielle.

"Leave them in the principal's office. You can pick them up on the way to the rink this afternoon. See you later. I want to hear all about Alex at lunch, though, and let me know what happens if you get to talk to Kyle," Danielle said, then scooted down the hall.

Nikki checked her watch and groaned. Fortunately most of the teachers in school understood that being in Silver Blades meant running late for classes. But she didn't want to push her luck with Ms. Purcell, her homeroom teacher.

As she turned to leave her locker, she heard a voice from behind. "Where'd those balloons come from?"

"Kyle!" Nikki's face lit up. "Am I glad to see you."

He didn't look half as glad as she felt. He seemed a little confused. He also kept staring at the balloons.

"They're from Alex," Nikki blurted out. She hadn't wanted to tell Kyle who'd sent them, but what else could she do? Eventually everyone in school would find out, and if she lied to Kyle, it would only make things worse.

"Uh, he must have brought them to school this morning," she went on, fumbling for words. Her voice was sort of high and squeaky, just as it always was when she was nervous. "We really aced this great move yesterday. . . ."

"And he sent you balloons to celebrate?" Kyle did not sound happy.

"I guess partners just do stuff like that." Nikki knew she sounded lame, but it was probably the truth.

Kyle shifted his beat-up black knapsack from his right shoulder to his left and stared down at his sneakers. When he looked up, he wore a sheepish grin. "Well," he said, raking his hand through his hair, "I guess that sort of makes sense." He met Nikki's gaze and smiled. "You deserve them. And, hey, I'm sorry I got so bent out of shape about that call waiting thing." He said it so sweetly that Nikki's heart stopped a minute. She felt herself start to blush again.

"So about Saturday," he continued. "We never did get to figure out how we're getting to that soccer game."

The soccer game! Nikki's mouth went dry. Her eyes rested on Alex's balloons. There was no way she could tell Kyle about going to the ballet with Alex.

Just then the third warning bell rang.

Kyle checked the clock at the end of the hall and looked a little worried. "Uh—we're going to be late for class," he said.

Nikki took a deep breath. She hated lying, but hurting Kyle seemed worse. "Kyle," she said, not quite able to meet his eyes. "I can't go."

"You can't?"

Nikki pushed her hair back from her face and took a deep breath. "I have too much homework this week. Skating has been taking up so much time, and my parents gave me this big lecture about grades. I have to stay home and study for two tests next Monday." Once she started telling her story, filling in the details was easy.

Much easier than watching Kyle's face. "Oh," he said. He looked so sad. For a second Nikki almost considered calling Alex and canceling their date for the ballet. But she couldn't. She just couldn't. It was the chance of a lifetime. Besides, Kathy Bart had said they should go. It was practically homework, like Alex said.

Kyle finally shrugged. "I understand." He reached out and shyly touched her cheek, then hurriedly stuffed his hand back in the pocket of his baggy jeans. "Parents are like that sometimes." He brightened a little. "So next time, then?"

"Right, next time." Nikki studied her shoes. Even though Kyle believed her, she had a terrible feeling in the pit of her stomach as she ran down the empty hall to class.

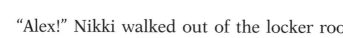

"Alex!" Nikki walked out of the locker room at the ice arena that afternoon and spotted her partner right away.

He was propped on the arm of one of the seats in the stands, talking to an auburn-haired girl Nikki had seen around before. She looked like a ninth- or tenth-grader and was wearing a purple Hawley Prep sweater. One of Alex's many fans, Nikki thought, and grinned. Alex had lots of pretty girl admirers.

"Nikki!" He waved, then said something to the girl and headed for Nikki. He was carrying a brown paper sack in one hand. "I've been looking for you." Nikki couldn't help noticing that Alex's blue sweater made his dark hair look even darker.

"Me too," Nikki replied, smiling. "Thanks for the balloons, but you shouldn't have done that."

Alex looked puzzled. "Why not? You're my partner and you were amazing yesterday."

"Uh, right," Nikki said. "It was really nice, but it seemed a little . . ." She wasn't sure if she should explain that sending balloons had made Kyle jealous.

"And I picked these up for you from the pro shop," Alex said before she could continue.

He offered Nikki the brown paper sack. Inside were her skates. She had left them at the shop to be sharpened. The silver blades above the skateguards gleamed.

"Thanks . . . again," she said, feeling flustered. "You really didn't have to do this."

"No big deal. Partners take care of each other."

"Okay, then," Nikki agreed. "That means I have to do something for you too."

"But you have," Alex said sincerely. "You're the perfect partner." He reached out and hugged her.

It was just a friendly squeeze, but Nikki instantly pulled away. She wondered how Alex always managed to be so casual and at the same time so sure of himself. She'd never skated pairs before. She still didn't know quite how to act around her partner or what all his attention meant.

Nikki tried to sound businesslike. "We've got to warm up now, don't we?"

Suddenly a voice cut right across the rink. "How could you do this to me?" It was practically a scream.

Nikki and Alex spun around in unison. "What's happening?" Alex asked.

"It's Haley," Nikki answered. "Look, she's really upset about something."

Haley was standing by the barrier, face-to-face with Michael. She was still in her practice clothes, though she had already taken off her skates. She stood in stockinged feet staring up at Michael. He had already changed into jeans and a sweater. And he looked very pale.

Haley did not look pale. Her face was as red as her hair, and her small hands were balled up into two tight fists. She looked as if she were either going to punch Michael or burst into tears—Nikki couldn't tell which.

"I thought we were supposed to stick together," Haley cried out. "Through thick and thin. Right to the end, Michael Bass." Haley's voice quavered, then she burst into a loud sob and raced past Nikki into the locker room.

6

"**H**aley, don't leave," Michael shouted, starting to follow her. Kathy Bart, who'd been standing a few feet away, pulled him back. "Not now. Let her go," she said. "Come into my office, and let's have a talk." She pushed him toward her small office, which was sandwiched between the snack bar and the pro shop.

Nikki looked from Kathy to the locker room to Alex. He looked really upset.

"Haley never cries," Alex said. He was right, Nikki thought. Haley always toughed it out. Even when her favorite coach had quit two days before a big competition and she and Michael had to start working with Kathy, Haley didn't cry.

"I wonder what's up," Nikki whispered to Alex.

"Hey!" Kathy shouted. "Nikki, get yourself on that ice and get warmed up. NOW," she barked. "You, too,

Alex. Your lesson will start in ten minutes. Get ready. I'll be right back."

Ordinarily when Kathy gave orders, Nikki didn't hesitate. But today she just couldn't get on the ice as her coach had commanded. Haley had looked so upset—Nikki wanted to see if she could help. After all, Haley was the reason why she and Alex had had such a good practice yesterday.

Seeing Nikki's hesitation, Alex reached out a hand. "Sarge is on the warpath," he warned. "We'd better get going."

But Nikki didn't take his hand. "I'll be right back." She peeled off her skating gloves and went to the locker room. The sound of Haley's muffled sobs floated out as she opened the door.

"Haley?" Nikki turned the corner and saw Haley sitting on the floor with her back against the mirror, her legs drawn up to her chest. Her face was buried in her arms, and her thin back shook with sobs.

"Are you okay?" Nikki asked softly. She wasn't sure what to do. "Do you want me to leave?"

Haley mumbled something into her knees, then looked up. Tears streamed out of her huge brown eyes. She looked miserable.

Nikki dropped down on the floor next to her. "Do you want to talk about it?" she asked, and pulled some tissues out of her sleeve. She handed them to Haley.

Haley took the tissues and blew her nose, then took

a shaky breath. "It's Michael," she said. "He's not going to skate with me anymore."

Nikki's jaw dropped. "What?"

"He's outta here in two weeks," Haley said. "Do you believe it? After we took that gold?"

Slowly Haley's words sank in. "Michael's really not skating with you anymore? But you're so great together. Why would he split up with you?"

Haley balled up her tissue and tossed it toward the nearest trash can. "He didn't. His dad got transferred. To Japan."

"That's halfway around the world!"

"Right." Haley looked so sad that Nikki wanted to reach out and hug her. "There's no way I can skate with him again."

Nikki refused to believe it. "There's got to be a way. Maybe Michael can find a place to stay here. Room with some family. Kathy or Mr. Weiler could arrange it."

"Forget it," Haley said, yanking off her sweater. She squirmed out of her tights and grabbed her jeans from her locker. "Mr. Bass won't let Michael stay here. Where the family goes, Michael goes. His dad's already found a top coach for him in Japan. By the time they get there, the coach will probably have a new partner lined up for Michael."

Nikki was speechless. She knew it wasn't easy to find a partner—someone the right size, weight, and at the right skating level who lived in the area. Let alone a really *good* partner. She had no idea what she'd do without Alex or how she'd ever skate pairs with anyone else.

Haley began pulling everything out of her locker. Tapes, socks, warm-ups, baseball caps, sweaters. She stuffed it all into her skate bag. When her skate bag was full, she began jamming the rest of her gear into her backpack.

Tears brimmed from her eyes as Haley turned to Nikki. "So I guess this is it for me too. I'm finished as a skater."

"Oh, don't say that," Nikki said softly. She put a hand on Haley's arm. "You're too talented. You'll find another partner. Kathy will track down someone for you, I know it."

"No way," Haley countered. "I've had other partners. Believe me. It's nearly impossible to find a good partner. You'll see. If you ever lose Alex, you'll know how I feel." She choked off a sob, pushed past Nikki, and ran out the door, just as Kathy stormed in.

Kathy whipped around. "Haley!" she shouted after her. The locker-room door swung back and forth behind her.

Kathy stared after Haley for a moment, then shook her head. She turned to Nikki. "And what do you think you're doing?"

Nikki cringed. "Haley was so upset . . . ."

"That is not your business right now," Kathy said in a quiet but stern voice. "It's bad enough my top pairs couple just split up. Now my second best couple isn't practicing."

Kathy held open the door. "Go practice!"

When Nikki hit the ice a few minutes later, she had a hard time concentrating. Everyone had thought that Michael and Haley's partnership was forever. Nikki herself had never imagined them breaking up.

"What happened?" Alex asked in a whisper. He took Nikki's hand, and she noticed his palm was a little sweaty. For the first time since she met him, Alex actually seemed nervous.

Nikki motioned with her head toward Kathy. The Sarge was talking to Mr. Weiler over by the sound system. Alex matched Nikki's long strokes around the arena. He didn't talk again until they were clear across the rink from the coaches. "Is Haley all right?" he asked.

"Haley and Michael broke up," Nikki said as she completed a footwork sequence. It sounded so final and real to say it out loud.

Alex skidded to a halt. He hung back by the barrier, just staring at her.

"Come off it!" He actually laughed. "That's crazy."

"It's true."

"Just like that? They broke up?"

"It's not like they had a fight or anything," Nikki said. She quickly explained about Michael's dad.

"That's pretty rotten for them," he said. He skated in a circle around Nikki. "But it wasn't like something went wrong between them." He looked at Nikki. "I couldn't stand it if we ever broke up."

"I'd be pretty upset too," Nikki admitted truthfully.

Alex took Nikki's hand. "Now's our chance to prove ourselves, Nikki," he said, making her look him in the eyes. "We're Silver Blades' only pairs team as of right now. And we'd better get our act together. The Sarge is watching. So is everyone else."

"Okay," Nikki agreed. "Let's do it." She pushed off with her skating leg and went into the preparation for the press lift that was the first part of their combination. Nikki helped Alex lift her with a good push off the ice. Her legs were strong, and the lift went perfectly. Nikki's arms were straight as she leaned back against Alex's body.

Suddenly, out of the corner of her eye, Nikki got a glimpse of Michael leaving the ice rink, lugging all his gear.

Just as Alex brought her down for her landing, her concentration broke, and she crashed hard on her rear. "Ouch!" she yelped.

"Nikki!" Alex shouted, and skated over to her.

But she was already on her feet, rubbing her bottom. "I'm okay," she assured him, testing her legs. She was bruised and would be several shades of purple in an hour or two, but she was used to falling.

"Focus, Nikki," Kathy called out, skating toward them. "You're not focusing. Time for your lesson. Are you guys ready to work?"

Nikki and Alex both nodded, and Alex crossed the ice to put their music tape into the cassette deck. Nikki watched him and breathed a sigh of relief. At least she and Alex were still together as a pairs team. She loved skating with him. They really were made for each other.

"You didn't have to *lie* to Kyle about the ballet," Danielle told Nikki early that evening as the two girls walked their bikes up the sweeping drive in front of Haley's house. They were on a mission to cheer up Haley. Tori had phoned them after dinner and told them to meet her there.

"But what could I do?" Nikki asked. "I know Kyle's jealous of Alex."

They parked their bikes next to Tori's and headed to the front door. Before Nikki had a chance to ring the bell, the door popped open.

"Welcome to the Museum!" Haley greeted them herself. She still looked pale but was calmer now. "Sorry I caused such a scene at the rink." Haley dug her bare toes into the thick white rug of the foyer. "But thanks for coming over. I can really use my friends."

"Hey, it's okay." Nikki hesitated a moment, then hugged Haley. Danielle patted Haley's shoulder.

Haley grinned at them, then crinkled her nose. "So let's head for my room. Tori's up there already. Don't step on the rug," she warned, making a face. "Mom hates dirt on her white rug."

"This place is really cool!" Danielle said as she and Nikki followed Haley up the broad spiral staircase.

"I've never been to a house with so much real art. No wonder you call it the Museum!"

Nikki tiptoed up the stairs afraid she might break something.

Tori was sitting on the floor in Haley's room. On a *patch* of floor was more like it. Nikki couldn't believe what a mess Haley's room was. Clothes were strewn everywhere, and Haley's skating gear was heaped at Tori's feet. Nikki watched as Tori neatly folded one of Haley's sweatshirts and carefully placed it back in the skate bag.

"I think I've convinced Haley to skate again," Tori said proudly.

"So you're not quitting Silver Blades?" Nikki asked Haley.

Haley shook her head. "No. I love skating too much to quit. I told my parents about Michael. They were disappointed, but they think I can do well at singles."

"Just what I told her too," Tori said.

Haley sighed. "It's better than not skating at all. But it sure's going to feel pretty crummy." She turned to Nikki, who was sitting on a black beanbag chair. "You know how skating alone feels, Nikki. Like half of you is missing."

Nikki nodded. "I don't think you should give up pairs. Kathy won't have trouble finding you another partner."

"I'm planning to talk to Kathy tomorrow. It's just that I don't think any new partner could be half as cool as Michael. He's a real friend." Haley sat on her bed and put her chin in her hands. "Maybe *was* a real friend is more like it."

"Michael's not angry with you," Danielle pointed out.

"He might be. I acted horrible at the rink today. He's probably never going to talk to me again."

Tori balled up a pair of Haley's tights and threw them at her. "That's ridiculous. He's going to miss you as much as you miss him."

"He probably feels as bad as you do—maybe even worse," Nikki suggested. "He has to leave all his friends in Seneca Hills and start all over in Japan."

"I know," Haley said. "I was thinking about how awful it would be to leave everyone I know and move so far away. I wish I could do something for him."

Tori jumped up. "Hey, I've got it! A party. We'll throw him a going-away party he'll never forget."

"Cool!" Nikki and Danielle exclaimed in unison.

"Where?" Haley asked, sounding skeptical. "My mother will never, and I mean *NEVER* let me have a party in our house."

"Right," Tori said, flopping down next to Haley on the bed. "Small detail. If Michael weren't leaving so soon, we could have it at my house," she said. "But my mother is busy right now with her business. She has a big fashion show coming up. She won't let me have a party now either."

"I've got it!" Danielle suddenly spoke up. "We could have the party at Kent Academy—if the school would let us."

"Dani, you're a genius," Tori exclaimed. "That's it. I'll call Ms. Carmichael, the headmistress, tomorrow."

"But he's leaving a week from next Wednesday," Haley moaned. "There's no time for a party."

"Oh, yes, there is," Tori said, sounding definite. She reached for some paper. "We can have a big picnic on Sunday for the whole school. Ms. Carmichael will love it. Let's make a list of all of Michael's other friends too."

"You guys all have to come." Haley turned to Nikki. Her cheeks were pink again and her eyes were shining.

"We'll be there!" Nikki assured Haley.

"I wouldn't miss it for the world," Danielle said. "Can Jordan and Kyle come?" she asked. She gave Nikki a meaningful look.

"Sure, everyone. It'll be a good chance to get the Kent kids together with some of the Grandview crowd—" Before Haley finished her sentence, the phone rang. She dove under a pile of clean laundry and pulled out her portable phone.

"Michael!" she yelled. "It's you. I'm so sorry I blew my cool today." She grinned at her friends, then motioned that she was going into the hall to talk to him alone.

"That party's a great idea," Nikki said to Tori. "You're a real friend," she said warmly.

"Of course!" Tori said, beaming at the compliment.

7

"**I** didn't think you'd get this upset," Alex whispered. It was Saturday afternoon, and the matinee performance of *Romeo and Juliet* was almost half over.

Nikki managed to locate a fistful of tissues. She suddenly felt embarrassed. "I'm not upset. I love it. It's just so sad."

No matter how many times she saw the love story and the dancing, she cried. She'd practically worn out her video of *Romeo and Juliet*. Nikki had never seen anything so beautiful as the *pas de deux* between the hero and heroine. The complicated steps and lifts looked easy and graceful, but Nikki knew from her own skating with Alex how hard the two dancers were working—how much strength and years of practice such effortless dancing took. She hoped someday she and Alex could skate that beautifully together too.

The house lights went up for the last intermission, and Nikki and Alex got up from their seats.

"You should have warned me," Alex joked. "I would have worn a raincoat."

Nikki laughed. Then she realized Alex had his arm around her. She eased out of his reach by shifting her purse higher up on her shoulder and holding her program with both hands.

Alex didn't seem to notice Nikki's reaction. "Did you see those lifts? The ones before Romeo leaves her? I was thinking we could try something like that in our program. We can try to block it out in the dance studio next week. Kathy'll love it."

The lifts. Right. Nikki breathed a sigh of relief, though she couldn't remember exactly what lift Alex was talking about. But she wanted to keep Alex talking about skating. Most of all she wanted to keep Alex from putting his arm around her.

"Hey, there's your dad!" Nikki spotted the tall, dark-haired man over by the staircase leading to the box seats. He was deep in conversation with a group of well-dressed people. "Didn't your dad say to meet him during the last intermission?"

"He looks too busy now. Want to get a soda?" Alex offered. He hurried to the refreshment stand and paid for their sodas before Nikki could even find the money her mother had given her. They went outside on the patio and sat down on a bench near a splashing fountain.

"Speaking of lifts," Alex said cheerfully, "the gloom

has lifted in the Haley-Michael department." He paused to chuckle at his joke. "I heard that you, Tori, and Dani came up with the idea for Haley to throw the going-away party at Kent Academy tomorrow."

"Yeah," Nikki said. Just thinking about the party tied her stomach in knots. Kyle would be there. So would Alex.

All week long Nikki had had to keep lying to Kyle about the weekend. She had to pretend she was half grounded and studying for her tests. She prayed every night he wouldn't find out she'd been lying. He'd be so hurt.

"I think Haley will find a new partner soon," Alex said, sounding very sure of himself. "She's small, agile, and already a champ. Lots of guys would love to skate with her. Kathy should have no problem once the word gets out that Haley's available. Of course finding the perfect partner might take some time."

Nikki nodded. "I'm glad Haley's going to skate pairs again. At first she was talking about doing singles training."

"But you know what our problem with pairs is?" Alex suddenly asked.

"Our death spiral?"

Alex shook his head, smiling. "All we ever talk about is skating." He squashed his empty soda can between his hands. He got up and tossed it in a recycling bin. "The problem is, I don't know anything about *you*."

She glanced up at him and replied cautiously, "What do you want to know?"

"I've got it. Let's tell each other three things about ourselves. But don't even mention the word *skating*. You first." He gave her arm a friendly poke.

Nikki glanced nervously at Alex. She definitely did not like the direction this conversation was headed. "You first. This is your idea, not mine."

"Okay. That's fair." He paused dramatically and pretended to think. Then he leaned close to Nikki. "I have a dog. His name is Barney."

"You do?" Nikki could feel her shoulders relax. She had never imagined Alex with a pet before. "I love dogs." She sighed and looked down at her shoes. "I used to have one. His name was Rocky. He was a Saint Bernard. He got hit by a car just before we left Missouri." Her voice caught in her throat.

"That's tough," Alex said. "You must really miss him."

Nikki nodded.

"Barney's having puppies," Alex said.

"That's the second thing I'm supposed to know about you?" Nikki couldn't help but laugh.

Alex swung one leg over the bench to face her. "No. But maybe you'd like one. Actually it's a friend's dog who's having the puppies, but since Barney's the father, we get to keep one if we want. My dad says our place is too small for two dogs."

"Sure. I'd love a puppy." She swung her feet back and forth and savored the idea for one whole minute. Her house often felt empty without Rocky. "But my parents probably won't go for it. They said something about a dog after we're more settled. Lately nothing looks settled. Mom's even repacking our trunks."

"You're moving?" Alex asked, looking worried.

"No." Nikki shook her head. "Once was bad enough. It's been hard getting used to living in Seneca Hills and not Missouri. But I've made lots of good friends this year."

"And skating with Silver Blades turned out great," Alex reminded her.

Nikki agreed. "But something is weird at home," she added. "My parents have both been off in the ozone lately." She creased her forehead and thought for a minute. "When we first moved here, they were all excited about Silver Blades and interested in my progress. Lately they haven't been asking about it at all, and Mom's been letting Mrs. Panati do all the carpooling back and forth from the rink. Mom's usually big on sharing stuff like that. But she's been sleeping late constantly. Maybe that's the problem. I've been leaving before she gets up, and half the time she's in bed or conked out on the sofa when I get home from the rink. We never see each other anymore."

"Doesn't sound like much of a problem," Alex remarked. "My dad's always on my case . . . though we get along pretty well," he hurried to add. "But I guess I'd worry a little if he sort of let up on me. You know how it is. You're an only child too."

"Yeah," Nikki said. "I'm almost always the center of attention. And now I miss it." She laughed self-consciously. "Why am I telling you this?"

"Because we're supposed to be getting to know each other better." Alex's dimples deepened as he smiled. "That's the best part about today." He slung his arm around her shoulder.

Nikki bent down to tighten the strap on her shoe and slipped out of his reach.

Alex seemed unfazed. He stretched his arms above his head and jumped up to stand on the the bench. He balanced for a minute, winked at Nikki, then jumped down gracefully. "You know, Nikki, Haley and Michael didn't just know each other on the rink. They were real friends. They had fun off the rink too. That's what made them really good partners. That's what I want for you and me."

"Me too," Nikki said firmly. "I want to be partners, like them. Partners and *friends*."

"Alex!" Mr. Beekman's voice came from somewhere behind them.

"Hi, Dad," Alex said, standing up. Nikki stood too.

"Having a good time?" Mr. Beekman asked. His smile was warm, and he had dimples just like Alex.

"Excellent, Dad," Alex said. Nikki nodded her agreement.

"Aren't you going to introduce me to your girlfriend?" Mr. Beekman asked. He gave Alex a hearty slap on the back.

Girlfriend? Nikki cringed.

"Nikki Simon . . ." Alex said, not bothering to deny a thing. "My dad—David Beekman."

At that moment the intermission bell rang. It was time to get back to their seats.

"See you kids later," Mr. Beekman said.

"Nice to meet you," Nikki called to Mr. Beekman. As they headed back inside, she didn't even look at Alex. She couldn't believe he would let his father think she was his girlfriend—especially after she'd just made a point of saying she wanted to be friends.

Alex started down the aisle ahead of Nikki, toward their seats. She followed him, mumbling at his back, "I'm *just* your partner." But Alex didn't answer. As the conductor raised his baton to signal the start of the last act, Nikki wasn't even sure Alex had heard her.

8

'This is the coolest going-away bash anyone has ever had. I just wish it weren't for Michael," Haley told Nikki, Tori, and Danielle the next afternoon at the Kent Academy picnic. Her face went from happy to sad. A softball sailed from the direction of the playing fields. Haley neatly snagged it. She tossed it back toward the diamond, and her smile was bright again.

Michael's farewell picnic was a big success. His whole eighth-grade class from Kent had turned up, as well as many of Haley's Silver Blades friends. The green lawn of the hilly campus was dotted with groups of kids eating, playing volleyball, and just hanging out near the barbecue in front of the stately stone administration building. Looking around, Nikki was sure she was the only person who wasn't having much fun.

She was still annoyed at Alex for acting as if she

were his girlfriend at the ballet. And all through Tori's guided tour of the sprawling Kent Academy campus, Nikki kept looking for Kyle. He hadn't turned up yet. She'd called him that morning to try to tell him about going to the ballet with Alex. She'd decided that lying to Kyle felt terrible and would only make the situation worse. But Kyle's hockey coach had scheduled an extra practice, and Kyle was running late. He'd barely had a minute to talk.

"How did your dream date go?" asked Danielle. She stooped to tie her sneaker.

"What dream date?" Haley asked.

Tori shrugged. "Dani's convinced that Alex is in love with Nikki." She cracked a smile at Nikki. "You gotta admit—sending you balloons and taking you to *Romeo and Juliet* is pretty romantic."

"It wasn't a date," Nikki insisted. "Alex and I are just friends. Besides, the Sarge more or less ordered us to go once Alex said he could get tickets. And it *was* helpful for a pairs team to watch those dancers perform those lifts."

"Does Alex know it wasn't a date?" Danielle persisted.

"I don't know what Alex thinks," Nikki said a bit sharply. "I only know that we're just partners. I'm already dating Kyle."

"Doesn't Alex know that?" asked Haley.

Nikki stared at Haley, wide-eyed. "I guess so. I don't really know." Suddenly she wished she had shared that fact with Alex yesterday. Maybe he didn't realize that she and Kyle were dating. Maybe Alex hadn't even noticed Kyle was jealous last week after Alex had pulled her ponytail.

As Nikki and her friends headed toward the two rows of picnic tables, Tori asked, "Does Kyle know you went out with Alex? You said you were going to tell him the truth."

Nikki sighed. "No, I didn't get a chance. But I will tell him the truth as soon as I see him. It's not fair to lie to him, and I'm really sorry that I ever did." She joined the line of kids filing toward the grill. "I just hope Kyle doesn't find out from somebody else. I want to be the one to tell him."

"We won't say anything," Tori said quickly. Danielle nodded agreement.

"My lips are sealed," Haley said.

"How will you eat?" Alex butted in as he came up behind the girls.

Haley groaned loudly.

Alex offered a plate to Nikki. "Want a hot dog?"

Nikki rolled her eyes. "Sure . . . but you didn't have to get it for me," she said as Mr. Carmichael, the headmistress's husband, put a hot dog and bun on her plate. "I'm not helpless." Nikki didn't mean to sound so sarcastic, but the last thing she needed today was Alex hanging around her when Kyle turned up.

"No problem," Alex said, but Nikki detected a hurt note in his voice. He followed her to the picnic table. Nikki started to pour herself a soda, but Alex beat her to it.

"Alex!" she protested. She glanced past his shoulder, looking for Kyle.

"What's with you?" he asked. "Didn't you have a good time yesterday?"

"Of course I did. I really loved the ballet."

Alex suddenly looked up and grinned. "Yo, Michael! You should leave town more often," Alex joked. "This is a really hot bash."

"Party on! How was the ballet yesterday?" Michael asked.

"Uh—great," Nikki said, feeling dismayed. Did everyone know about the ballet already? She looked toward the parking lot to see if Mrs. Panati's Volvo had pulled up with the guys from the Hawks practice.

"*Great* isn't the word for it," Alex chimed in. "You should check it out sometime. But if you take your partner to see *Romeo and Juliet*, be sure and wear a raincoat. It's a tearjerker. Nikki cried so much, she ruined my jacket."

"She did what?"

Kyle's voice shot through Nikki like a sliver of ice. She whirled around. Kyle was standing there staring at her. His green-and-white Hawks gym bag was slung over his shoulder, and his eyes were wide with disbelief.

"Uh-oh," Nikki heard Danielle murmur.

"How about a hamburger?" Tori suggested, stepping up to Kyle.

But Kyle stood frozen, glaring at Nikki. "What did he say, Nikki?"

Nikki opened her mouth to speak, but no words would come out. She'd never been so mortified in her life.

"We were just talking about the ballet yesterday," Alex piped up. "Nikki and I checked it out, and—"

"You were at the ballet yesterday?" Kyle looked from Nikki to Alex, then back at Nikki.

Nikki forced herself to look him in the eyes. "It's not what you think, Kyle."

"Then why did you tell me you were studying?" he demanded. "What am I supposed to think?"

Alex straightened up a little. "What's going on?" he asked Nikki.

"Good question," said Kyle.

Nikki's voice shook. "Kyle, listen to me."

"Why? So you can lie to me again?"

"I just didn't want to hurt your feelings."

"So you lie and go out with another guy and tell me you're studying." Kyle's voice broke slightly as he jammed his fists into the pockets of his team jacket.

"I wasn't out with another guy . . . not like that. . . . It wasn't a date," Nikki said with a shaky voice. "You know that Alex is just my partner."

"Gimme a break!" Kyle cried. "I'm not *that* stupid. You already spend half your days with him. If you aren't dating Alex, then why lie about it?"

Nikki glanced pleadingly at Alex. He had to say something, anything, to let Kyle know he had the wrong idea about them.

But Alex just stood there, rocking back and forth on

his heels, his hands stuffed in his jeans pockets. He avoided Nikki's eyes. She couldn't believe it. He wasn't going to help her.

"I'm outta here!" Kyle finally snapped, and turned on his heel.

"Kyle . . ." Nikki called after him, but she knew it was hopeless. Kyle was walking away from the picnic and away from her, and it didn't look as if he'd be back anytime soon.

9

As soon as Nikki could swallow the tears gathering in her throat, she marched up to Alex, her fists balled up at her sides. She planted herself in front of him so that he had to look at her. He seemed surprised when he saw how angry she was.

"Why did you do that?" she accused. Her voice trembled. "This is all your fault."

"Why did I do *what*?" Alex demanded. "What's all my fault?"

"Why didn't you speak up and tell Kyle the truth?" Nikki cried.

"Nikki," she heard Tori start to warn her.

Then Danielle pulled Tori away. "Let's let Nikki handle this herself," Danielle whispered, and the two of them edged their way farther down the table. Haley and Michael went with them.

Nikki forced her attention back on Alex. "So, why? Why did you let Kyle think we were on a date?" She glared at Alex.

"I'm not the one who lied to him. You can't blame me for whatever's going on with you two."

"It's not what's going on with me and Kyle that's the problem. It's you. You could have just told him we were only partners."

"Why should I?" Alex retorted. "Everyone knows that. I can't help it if you're afraid to tell the truth because your boyfriend is jealous. What is your problem?"

"You, Alex!" Nikki actually screamed. "You."

Alex slowly shook his head. "You're the one with the problem. You're the one who lied. You can't lay it on me." He kicked the grass and stomped off toward the baseball field.

Hot, angry tears spilled out of Nikki's eyes. She bolted toward the ivy-covered student union to call home. She was furious and hurt and embarrassed.

She had never yelled at someone so loudly in public before. But at the moment she didn't care. She only wished she could blast off and move to some planet that didn't contain Alex. She couldn't imagine ever speaking to him, let alone skating with him again. She hated Alex Beekman. She hated him, hated him, hated him. He had just ruined her life and he had the nerve to say it was all her fault.

Inside the student union Nikki searched for a pay phone. She finally found a phone booth by the girls' bathroom.

Nikki headed toward it, fumbling in her purse for change. She tried to calm herself down, to stop crying. She didn't want to sound so out of control that her mother thought she'd had some kind of an accident or something.

She popped her quarter in the slot and sniffed back her tears. She cleared her throat as she dialed her number. She was going to ask her mother to pick her up and take her right home. She'd meet her by the side gate. That way she wouldn't have to face the other kids at the picnic. She wasn't sure how she'd face them all again.

The phone rang and rang. Then it stopped.

"You have reached the Simon residence. We can't come to the phone right now, but if you leave your name and . . ."

Nikki slammed down the receiver so hard, the partition of the phone booth shook. She pressed her back against the wall. Why weren't her parents around when she needed them?

Nikki allowed herself to cry another minute, then she squared her shoulders and headed for the door. Even if she couldn't get a ride home, there was no way she was going to hang around this picnic one minute longer waiting until Mrs. Panati picked her up at five.

She started walking down the long driveway in front of the school. Then she heard footsteps behind her. Nikki hoisted her bag higher up on her shoulder and broke into a run. She didn't want anyone to try to stop her.

"Hey, wait for us!" Tori shouted.

"Nikki," Danielle called.

Nikki came to a stop. She took a deep breath before she turned around. Haley was with Tori and Danielle. Nikki was too embarrassed to look her friends in the eyes.

Tori had retrieved her pocketbook and was putting on her sweater. Danielle was carrying her Silver Blades club jacket. Haley had her baseball bat and mitt. They were all leaving the picnic. Because of her. "You guys didn't have to leave," Nikki mumbled, digging the toe of her loafer into the ground.

Tori straightened her headband, then gently tugged the skate charm Nikki wore around her neck and smiled. "We're your friends, remember? We're not going to hang out here while you're off by yourself."

"That's right," Danielle agreed firmly, hooking one arm through Nikki's. "Even if that means leaving the picnic and going home with you."

"Michael's had enough of me by now," Haley added. "He's hanging out with the kids from his class."

Nikki stared at her friends. When she had first moved to Seneca Hills, it had been hard to leave behind the friends and coach she had known for years. But somehow the girls in Silver Blades had become even closer friends in such a short time. Maybe it was because they spent so much time training so hard at the rink. Whatever it was, Tori, Danielle, and Jill always helped her to feel better when she was upset.

"Thanks, guys," Nikki said softly. "I'm not sure I deserve such good friends, especially after what I did to Kyle."

"You *don't* deserve us," Tori kidded.

"But we're stuck with you!" said Danielle.

"Like glue," Haley agreed, linking her arm through Nikki's. "Now, where to?"

As the four of them headed for the bus stop and home, Nikki was happy to realize she counted Haley as a real friend too.

That night after dinner Nikki was determined to try to talk to her mom. Nikki felt rotten about losing her boyfriend. And she wondered if she had blown her pairs partnership with Alex by having a fight with him. She hoped a heart-to-heart with her mom would help her sort out this mess. Her mom had always helped her through problems in the past.

Nikki went into the living room. Her parents were there, talking. As soon as Nikki walked in, the talking stopped.

Nikki groaned softly. Here we go again. This had happened last night and the previous afternoon. In all her thirteen years she had never seen her parents have so many private conversations.

"Niks?" Her father seemed surprised even to see her there.

Nikki shook her head in disbelief. "What's with you guys?" she said sharply. "Remember me? Nikki Charlotte Simon. Your daughter. I live here." She flopped down on the couch across from her parents.

Nikki stared at her mother and couldn't believe her eyes. Her mother was eating Super Chocolate Crunch ice cream—and right out of the container! Her nutrition-conscious mother almost never ate ice cream.

Nikki picked up a throw pillow and hugged it.

"Is something wrong, Nikki?" her mother asked.

"Yeah, I guess," Nikki said, twirling the fringe on the pillow. Suddenly she wasn't sure where to start. There was so much to tell them.

Her mother got up and put the ice cream on the coffee table. She sat down next to Nikki on the couch. "You look like you need a hug. I can certainly see that." She drew Nikki into her arms, and Nikki returned her mother's hug gratefully.

Then her mother tousled Nikki's hair and plopped back against the pillows on the couch. "We haven't seen each other much lately."

Nikki smiled with relief. "You've noticed too?"

"Are things okay at the rink?" her father asked.

"At the rink?" Nikki repeated. "Nothing's wrong at the rink . . . yet . . . ." Before she could say more, her mother broke in.

"That's good. But you know, you look awfully tired,

Nikki, and your eyes are a bit puffy. I think you need some sleep. You've got an early session tomorrow morning. Mrs. Carsen will be here at five to pick you up. You'd better head off to bed."

"Go to bed?" Nikki repeated numbly.

"You *do* look tired," her father added. "Too much fun at that picnic—"

"Yeah, right, the picnic, was a blast," she said glumly.

"I know, Niks," her father spoke up. "You'll miss Michael. It's hard when friends move. But you'll feel better after a good night's sleep."

She sighed, then got up. "Right. A good night's sleep can't hurt."

Nikki went up to her room and flopped onto her bed. She wished Michael's leaving really *was* the problem. Instead the problem was Alex.

10

"**W**e have to talk." Alex's voice behind her made Nikki jump.

It was five-thirty Monday morning, and the dimly lit rink was filled with the muffled sound of blades cutting into the fresh ice. A handful of skaters wove their way among the shadows, warming up for early practice. Nikki was slowly circling the rink, willing her legs to wake up. The rest of her wasn't very awake either. She stifled a yawn. She knew her eyes were red from lack of sleep and from all the crying she'd done.

"We have to be professional about this," Alex continued. "We have to act grown up. Whatever problems we have off the ice, here we forget them. I don't think either of us wants to risk our whole skating career because of some stupid argument." He sounded as if he had rehearsed his comments.

In the shadowy light she could see Alex's jaw was set. He's still upset, she realized. So was she. But his determination to act professional made her feel better and less angry at him.

She folded her arms across her chest and skated in a little circle as he talked.

"We'll work as if nothing happened," Alex said.

"It's a deal," Nikki agreed. "On the ice it'll be as if yesterday never happened. Let's stop talking and start skating."

Easier said than done, she thought half an hour later.

Halfway through their lesson Kathy was on their case. Big-time.

Not that Nikki could blame her. As Nikki fought to catch her breath, she actually wondered why Kathy hadn't completely hit the roof. All morning Nikki had continued to flub the very same star lift they had mastered a week ago.

"One more time," Kathy instructed. "Nikki, you're holding back today. Just go for it."

Nikki nodded, determined to get it right. She skated backward toward Alex. Her hand met his. His palm was sweaty when Nikki tried to jump, and his arm felt shaky. Then, halfway into the lift, his hand slipped. For the fourth time Nikki landed on her rear. "Arrrgh!" she groaned.

"You okay?" Alex sounded really worried as he reached out his hand. She took it, scrambled to her feet, and brushed herself off.

"Sure. I'm fine," she replied. "One more bruise to add to the collection," she joked, trying to ignore the fact that she had never fallen so many times during a lesson in six months of pairs skating.

"*Enough!*" Kathy yelled. "Lesson's over for today." Nikki looked at the clock. They weren't even halfway through their usual hour. Nikki skated over to the barrier and wiped off her skate blades with a rag, then put on her guards.

"Come over here!" Kathy ordered. She was propped on the arm of a seat, pouring coffee from her thermos.

"Okay, you guys," Kathy said brusquely. "You've just had the worst lesson of your life!" She looked from Alex to Nikki and shook her head. "Never again are you two to turn up for a lesson and skate this sloppily."

Kathy paused as if she expected them to say something. Nikki felt her face go red. For once Alex was at a loss for words too. He just stared at his skates.

"Sorry," Nikki finally mumbled, and glanced up at Kathy.

"We won't do it again," said Alex.

Kathy went on. "Today you skated as if you were two different people on the ice, performing your own singles programs. That's a disaster when it comes to pairs skating. Pairs is a team effort. If either one of you loses your concentration, the other one can get hurt." Kathy paused ever so slightly, then actually began to smile. "Of course partying too much the day before a lesson isn't so smart either. . . ."

"Partying too much?" Alex repeated, then glanced quickly at Nikki.

"Michael's going-away party. I'm sure it was fun, and you both look very tired. Just don't overextend yourselves off the ice again. Now and then it's fine, but sooner or later your skating will really suffer." Kathy checked her watch. "Time for school. But I expect you to have your act together by tomorrow."

Tomorrow! Nikki thought as she walked slowly to the locker room. She massaged the back of her neck and winced.

Today she felt like a perfect disaster on the ice, not a perfect partner. Having a fight with Alex had seemed to change everything between them . . . overnight! Moves that had seemed so easy only a couple of days ago suddenly seemed impossible.

Nikki changed for school and headed for the snack bar to get some juice while she waited for Tori and Danielle to finish their singles sessions. On the way past the rink she peered in the glass window of the rink door. Nikki watched as Tori leaped into a double lutz, twirling around in the air. Tori landed the difficult jump perfectly. Nikki envied her a moment. Singles suddenly seemed so much easier than pairs.

"It's getting worse and worse," Nikki told Haley a few days later in the weight room. She jerked the Velcro tabs that held the five-pound weights around her slender ankles. "I'm beginning to think pairs skating is a really big mistake for me. I've been flubbing every spin, every turn, every lift. . . . I'm even getting scared when Alex actually *does* manage to hang on to me and hold me over his head."

Nikki got to her feet, grabbed her towel, and wiped the beads of sweat off her face. "I used to love the feeling of being high in the air above his head. It used to feel like flying. Now I feel like I should be wearing a parachute in case I fall." She tried to joke, but even to her own ears her voice sounded strained.

"You're just going through a bad phase," Haley said. "Really, it happens to everyone. Michael and I would have weeks of awful skating, then suddenly poof!" She snapped her fingers in the air and grinned. "You'll see. Soon you'll be skating together better than ever."

"I don't know," Nikki said, rubbing her thigh. "If this goes on much longer, I won't have a part of me that *isn't* black-and-blue." She looked down at Haley. The smaller girl was lying on a tilt board doing sit-ups. "Haley," she said, squatting down on the floor beside her. "Sometimes, it feels as if Alex's dropping me on purpose."

Haley sat up abruptly. "No way!"

She looked so startled that Nikki laughed a little. "Well, maybe not, but it *feels* that bad—as if we don't trust each other anymore."

Haley hugged her knees to her chest and looked right at Nikki. "You've got to stop worrying all the time, or you're not going to be able to work up the nerve to go out there and do the lifts well together. Alex *has* been dropping you a lot, but your timing's been off too. Don't make such a big deal. You'll both get over it."

"Okay. I'll try. I'm sure you're right," Nikki said, standing up.

She walked out of the weight room—and right into Kyle. His arms were full of hockey sticks, and he was wearing his green-and-white Hawks helmet.

Nikki bumped into him so hard, the sticks clattered to the floor.

"Hey, watch it!" Kyle said.

"Sorry," Nikki mumbled, and forced herself to meet his eyes.

Kyle's expression was stony, and his blue eyes were cold with anger. Nikki's face felt hot. She stooped down quickly to hide her blush and to help him pick up the sticks.

"Don't bother," he grumbled. Nikki stayed crouched down beside him, not sure what to do. They hadn't exchanged a single word since the picnic on Sunday. She'd called him several times, but he was never home and didn't return the calls. She hadn't seen him once in school or at the rink. Nikki was sure Kyle had made himself scarce on purpose.

"Kyle, I'm sorry," she blurted out. "About Alex and—"

But Kyle wasn't about to give her a chance to apologize. He scooped up the sticks and turned his back. Then he marched across the lobby to the hockey rink.

Dragging her feet past the pro shop, Nikki entered the arena. She climbed into the bleachers to put on her skates. She quickly laced them up, then jammed on the earphones to her portable tape player and popped in her favorite tape. It was the one her friend Katy had made for her back in Missouri, with music meant to calm her down, center her.

She closed her eyes, leaned back in the seat, and breathed deeply.

"Ready?" Alex's brusque voice jarred her eyes open.

She took off her headphones. "I guess so." But her heart wasn't in it.

"Look, Kathy's on our case big-time. I don't think we should sit around listening to tapes. I think we should be skating." Nikki didn't miss the hostile note in his voice. "We need all the practice we can get."

"All right," Nikki snapped. "I'm ready. I'm ready."

She pulled off her skate guards and stepped onto the ice. Alex followed her.

"What do you think we should work on?" she asked, skating over to Alex.

"That death spiral."

"Do you think so?" Nikki felt a wave of doubt. Thanks to Haley's coaching, Nikki's death spiral had improved. But the move still scared her, especially when her head skimmed the ice as Alex spinned her around.

Alex nodded. "Why not?" He pulled off his sweatshirt and tossed it into the bleachers. He checked to see that their end of the rink was empty. "We haven't blown that one yet," she thought she heard him mumble.

Think positive, she told herself. She tried to picture exactly what the perfect death spiral should look like. Stay relaxed, she repeated again and again as she skated around the rink, trying to build up speed and power. But her knees felt like jelly. She wasn't sure she could trust Alex anymore to really hang on to her during the treacherous maneuver. But she had to try.

As Alex spun her faster and faster, she lay back until she was almost parallel to the ice. But her body was tense, and she felt her skating foot begin to wobble. At that moment Alex let go of her.

Nikki heard herself scream. Then her world went black.

11

"**N**ikki?" Voices floated somewhere far above Nikki's head.

She opened her eyes to a blur of light.

Then Kathy's face snapped into focus. So did the pain in Nikki's shoulder.

"Ooooh!" she moaned, lying on the ice. What had happened? She couldn't quite catch her breath to speak. She felt fuzzy and confused. She blinked. Behind Kathy was Mr. Weiler, Haley, Danielle, Tori. Everyone was leaning over her.

"Nikki?" Kathy's voice was extremely gentle. "Are you hurt?"

"No . . ." she said. "I don't think so." She wiggled her toes inside her skates and clenched and unclenched her fingers. Everything worked. "I—I'm okay. Nothing's broken." She forced herself to sit up and gingerly

88

rolled her neck. Her shoulder felt bruised, but she'd been bruised before.

Then she saw Alex. He was whiter than the ice. "Nikki?" He reached for her hand.

"You let go of me!" she cried, backing away. She tried to scramble to her feet.

Mr. Weiler's hand grabbed her elbow. "Easy. Easy. Are you okay?"

"Are you dizzy?" Kathy took her other arm and steered her over toward the bleachers.

"She just got the wind knocked out of her," Danielle said. "It was a hard fall."

"It wasn't just a fall." Nikki shot a piercing glance at Alex. "He dropped me." She began shaking all over. "He let go of me on purpose." Her mouth would barely form the words. "On purpose," she repeated in a very soft, very frightened voice.

Mr. Weiler looked shocked. "What are you saying?" He looked from Nikki to Alex and back to Nikki.

Nikki gulped down some air and just stared at her skating partner.

Alex returned her stare, stunned. He was speechless. He shook his head and skated away from the little knot of onlookers. Nikki watched him.

Kathy shook her head. "That's ridiculous." She put her hand under Nikki's chin and gently tilted her face up to look her in the eye. "Alex would not drop you or anyone on purpose. That's the silliest thing I've ever heard."

"No it's not," Nikki blurted. "All week, you've seen what's been going on—"

"Yes, I have," Kathy was firm now. She waved Mr. Weiler and the other people away from them. Then she motioned Alex over.

Alex folded his arms across his chest, set his jaw, glared at Nikki.

Kathy's voice was low and serious. Nikki couldn't tell if she was angry or annoyed or just really worried.

"All week long I have witnessed some of the sloppiest skating I have ever seen in this club from the two of you," she said. "You've both had your mind on everything but your skating.

"If you have some kind of problem, I'm here to help you—both of you. You are supposed to be a team. Pairs sometimes go through tough times. Maybe I've been working you twice as hard since Haley and Michael split up. I just thought you could take it." Kathy put down her coffee mug and considered both of them. "Until now you've shown the best sense of teamwork I've ever seen in kids your age."

"Teamwork?" Nikki couldn't stand it anymore. "We're no team. We aren't even talking to each other. He hates me," she blurted. "You can think whatever you want to, Kathy, but he let go of me. He just let go." Nikki didn't even bother to fight the tears rising to her eyes.

"How can you listen to her?" Alex turned on Kathy. "I didn't drop her. My hand slipped. It's not the first time that's happened. Nikki's the one who doesn't want to skate with me. She's been shying away from all the throws and jumps. Her heart's not in this anymore." He faced Nikki again. "And if you were the last pairs skater in the world, I'd never get on the ice with you again."

Alex pushed off forcefully onto the ice, his blades cutting into the surface.

"You don't have to," Nikki cried after him. "Because I'd be crazy to ever skate again with you."

"Nikki! Alex!" Kathy's voice called after her. But Nikki half limped, half ran into the locker room. Danielle was there, and Haley and Tori, but she turned her back on all of them. She pulled off her skates, jammed them in her locker, and yanked on her jeans right over her tights.

"Nikki, calm down," Haley urged. "It was an accident."

"He didn't drop you on purpose," Danielle said.

Nikki turned on both of them, furious. "You'd better believe he did. He's so angry about that fight that all he wants to do is get back at me."

Tori whistled softly. "You've worked too hard to just throw it all away. *Everyone* says you guys have what it takes."

Nikki clapped her hands over her ears. She didn't want to hear another word of this.

"I don't care what *everyone* says, Tori. I know what I feel. I'm never skating with *anyone* again. And if I didn't think it would give that creep too much satisfaction, I would quit skating altogether."

Nikki pushed past her friends and stomped out into the night. Rain poured down her face and mixed with her tears. She was supposed to be getting a ride home with Danielle, but no way was she waiting for Mrs. Panati. She didn't care if she got completely drenched. Besides, she sure wasn't in the mood to hear Danielle defend Alex. She'd take the bus.

She was halfway across the ice arena parking lot, when a red Mustang rolled up.

"Nikki!" Kathy called out the window. "Come on. You're going to get soaked, and then you'll be sick. You're overheated from practice. I'll give you a ride home."

Not now, Nikki wailed to herself, but she really didn't have a choice. Besides, Kathy was right. Every inch of her already ached. The cold rain would make her worse. Kathy opened the passenger door. Nikki climbed in. She snapped on her seat belt and stared straight ahead.

"Nikki," Kathy's voice was soft. "Don't make a snap decision about Alex. You should really sleep on this."

"This isn't a snap decision," Nikki said through her tears. "I've been thinking about it all week." And in a way she had, ever since that blowup at the picnic. "I can't trust him."

"Alex *didn't* drop you on purpose," Kathy said pointedly. "He said his hand slipped and you were off balance. I saw the whole thing." They stopped at a light, and Kathy turned to face Nikki. "Nikki, you haven't seemed yourself all week. What's wrong?"

"Everything," she said, thinking back on that afternoon's conversation with Haley. "Everything that has to do with skating pairs. I don't feel Alex and I work very well together anymore. We're not a good team. I've sort of lost my trust in him, I guess." As she spoke, Nikki replayed the fall in her head.

Kathy seemed to read her thoughts. "What happened today *was* an accident, Nikki," she said gently as the light turned to green and they started up the long hill leading to Nikki's neighborhood. "But if you start filling your head with all sorts of negative thoughts about skating pairs, it's bound to affect your performance on the ice sooner or later. Remember, half the sport of skating is psychological. If you make up your mind it won't work, well," Kathy concluded with a shrug, "it won't."

Nikki blew out her breath. After a moment's silence she said, "What happened today didn't *feel* like an accident. But even if it was, that doesn't change how I feel. I'm not skating with him again." She stared at her hands, and a thought formed in her head. "I'm not skating with *anyone* again. But I don't want to stop skating. I love it too much."

Kathy turned the corner onto Main Street. In the shadowy light Nikki could see that her lips were pursed. Nikki worked up her nerve to say what she was thinking. She wanted to be up front with Kathy.

"I want to skate singles again. Is it too late to pick up where I left off last fall?" Nikki had been taking two singles lessons a week, but most of her energy and concentration had been devoted to working with Alex as a pairs team. Well, she'd change that now . . . if Kathy would let her.

"No. It's not too late. You're a very talented skater. But your chance of making it in singles to the Nationals are very small. For every pairs team there are at least one hundred excellent ladies figure skaters. As I've been telling you, I think that you and Alex have a very good chance of making it to the top in pairs."

As Kathy pulled up to Nikki's house, she said, "This is your decision. But promise me you'll really talk this over with your parents and sleep on it."

Nikki promised. She knew she couldn't make a big skating change like this without her parents' input. But her own mind was made up already. With Alex out of the picture there would be no more arguments. No more games. And no more pretending he was her boyfriend. It would be a huge relief.

"Thanks for the ride," she said, and ran to the house through the rain.

12

'I have *not* changed my mind, Haley," Nikki insisted the following Saturday at the mall's Buckaroos Western shop. "I am never skating with Alex again. Ever. Besides, I've given up on pairs once and for all."

Nikki had gone to the mall partly to keep her promise to go shopping with Haley and partly just to have fun. But discussing Alex with Haley was definitely not fun.

"So what'd your parents say—you did tell them?"

Nikki nodded and said, "I told them, all right. It was the first time in weeks they actually sat down and listened to me. And they even had something to say about it." Nikki put her hands in her pockets of her denim jacket and leaned back against the mirrored wall. "Maybe I should get in big trouble more often. It seems to impress them."

Haley cracked up. "Whoa! Nikki Simon turns into a bad girl! Read all about it in the morning paper!"

It was Nikki's turn to laugh. One great thing about Haley was she tended to be upbeat almost all the time. Nikki was really starting to like her more and more. "Anyway," Nikki continued, as she idly pushed hangers full of Western-style skirts and vests down the rack. "They said it was my decision. They just wanted me to be happy. And to keep skating. They'll stick up for me, whatever I do."

"Well, that's cool," Haley said, holding up a denim vest.

"Try it on," Nikki urged, and started toward the dressing room.

"No. We have to talk," Haley suddenly said. She hung the vest back on the rack and steered Nikki out of the store.

"Haley," Nikki protested, laughing. "What's wrong?" She trotted after Haley.

Haley plopped down on a bench near the mall's atrium fountain. She patted the seat next to her. Nikki sat down.

"Now, don't get me wrong about this, but I wanted to clear it with you first, before I even mentioned it to Kathy," Haley said. Nikki had never seen her look so serious.

Haley looked directly into Nikki's eyes. "Are you really and truly are finished skating with Alex?"

Nikki groaned. "This is getting old, Haley. I told you that."

"You haven't got one itsy, bitsy, tiny doubt about your decision never to skate with him again?" Haley pressed.

"I—"

Haley stopped her. "Think a minute."

"I'm finished with Alex," Nikki declared.

"So you won't mind if I try skating with him?"

Nikki's mouth fell open. "You? With Alex Beekman?" She stared at Haley, waiting for the punch line, the trick spider to pop out from somewhere, the whoopee cushion to squeak. "You've got to be kidding."

"Nope." Haley sounded all-business. "I just don't want to mess things up for you if Alex and I start skating together." She paused, and looked at her feet. "I wouldn't do that to a friend."

Nikki didn't know what to say. "This is for real?"

"No joke," Haley replied.

"Hey," Nikki said with a casual shrug. "He's all yours." As she spoke, she remembered the time Haley had demonstrated that death spiral with Alex. Even without practice they had skated well together.

Haley bounced up and grinned down at Nikki. "All right!" she cheered, and reached out her hand to slap Nikki a high-five.

"I just hope it works out okay," Nikki said, trying to ignore the sinking feeling in her heart.

"I can't wait to see Kathy's face when I ask her." Haley was positively glowing now. "I just hate skating alone. It's no fun. You know how weird it feels when you're used to a partner. Tori and Dani don't seem to get it."

"I hope Mr. Weiler's in a better mood today," Tori grumbled on Monday morning as she and Nikki headed across the parking lot for the ice arena. The white building was pink with the dawn, and the grass surrounding it shone with thick dew. Nikki shivered inside her jacket as Tori stopped to wave at her mother. Nikki watched the silver Jaguar take off.

"Mr. Weiler's really been on my case," Tori complained. "He told me my camel spin looked more like a camel's hump."

Tori mocked her coach's thick German accent, and Nikki giggled.

"At least your mom won't be around today to see him complain," Nikki said.

Tori's rosy face lifted in a smile. "Mom's being pretty good about not playing rink mother—at least she doesn't come to practice every day anymore."

Nikki was happy to see that Tori's latest stab at solving her problems with her super-demanding mother seemed to be working out. Mrs. Carsen was very hard on Tori. Tori said it was because her mother was an ex-skater who gave up her chance at a professional skating career when she got married, and she had always regretted it.

At this moment Nikki wished her own skating were

up to Tori's level. Months of working at pairs had made her stronger at the things she was naturally good at—spins, footwork, and the more lyrical moves. But her jumps hadn't improved that much.

She had been thinking about Haley's plan to skate with Alex. She had told Haley it was cool and she meant it. She really did.

Yet, deep down inside, she felt as if she had lost something. And to make things even worse, Kyle still wasn't speaking to her. She had stuck an apology note in his locker at school a few days ago. She was sure he had found it. But he never said anything. Maybe she would write him another note. Somehow I have to make things okay between us, Nikki thought.

When she and Tori emerged from the locker room a few moments later, the rink was still fairly deserted. A couple of mothers sat high in the bleachers sipping coffee and reading morning papers. The sound of blades scraping the ice broke the hush of the arena.

Nikki walked down the rubber matting and tossed her towel and duffel onto a seat. As she held on to the railing and took off her skate guards, two shadows glided out of the dark of the rink, into the light.

Nikki froze.

Tori gasped. "Who's that with Haley?"

Nikki's voice sort of stuck in her throat. "Alex," she finally managed, not quite believing her eyes. The pair was skating hand in hand into the full light of the arena, and each of them went into a sit spin. Their line didn't quite match, and Alex was a hairline slower coming out of the spin than Haley.

"Not bad!" Tori remarked, and glanced at Nikki.

Nikki shrugged. We were better the first time we did that together, she couldn't help thinking.

"Nikki Simon, you're upset!" Tori sounded surprised. Then she reached out and touched Nikki's arm gently. "Hey, do you really want to be back with Alex?"

Nikki pulled her arm away. "Don't be ridiculous." She managed a weak smile.

Tori's eyebrows shot up. "Oh." Then she turned back toward the ice and remarked, "For two people who have never skated together before, Haley and Alex look pretty good to me. What's the big deal anyway? They both needed new partners." She lowered herself to the floor with her legs wide to do her stretches. "And you *did* announce to the whole world you never wanted to skate with him again."

"I don't!" Nikki replied. "And that's not the point." She dug her fists into the pockets of her warm-up jacket.

"Whatever," Tori said with a puzzled expression on her face.

Nikki grabbed the earphones to her Walkman and popped in the tape of the music Kathy had chosen for her singles program. She turned the volume up as loud as she could bear. She didn't want to discuss Alex with Tori anymore.

But as she began her own off-ice warm-up, she kept one eye on the rink.

Haley was roughing out the program she'd skated

with Michael for Alex. Nikki watched Haley coaching Alex, telling him which step, which jump, which spin was next. And every time Alex touched Haley's hand, or spun alongside her, or threw her into a jump, Nikki's whole body went through the move with Haley. Every muscle in her body seemed to remember what it felt like skating with Alex.

Haley looked so happy skating with someone again. Nikki truly wanted to feel happy for her. After all, Haley was supposed to be her friend. But instead Nikki felt left out and confused.

The shrill blast of Kathy's whistle cut right through the volume on Nikki's Walkman. Nikki pulled off her earphones.

"What's all this about?" Kathy murmured half to herself as she strode up to the barrier. She turned to Nikki. She held Nikki's gaze a moment. Nikki gave a little wave. She hoped she looked casual.

"Ready for your lesson?" Kathy asked. Nikki nodded. "Then start warming up, I'll be right with you." Kathy leaned over the barrier as Haley skated up.

To get onto the ice, Nikki had to slither past Alex. He just stood there as she squeezed by. Her cheeks burned. Then she bumped into Haley.

"Hi, Nikki!" Haley sounded a little worried.

"Uh, hi," was all Nikki could manage.

Kathy was obviously waiting to talk to Haley. "How did all this come about?" she asked her.

"Nikki said it was okay," Haley replied, looking embarrassed. "I mean, I asked her if—"

"So Nikki is assigning partners around here?" Kathy said.

"It's not up to me," Nikki said firmly, avoiding Alex's gaze. "I just told Haley that Alex and I weren't skating together anymore."

Haley looked relieved. "Right. And Alex and I both need partners, so we wanted to give it a try."

Kathy looked uncertain for a moment, but then agreed.

"Okay, we'll give it a shot. I'll schedule class time with you both this afternoon."

Alex mumbled something Nikki couldn't catch. She took her practice tape out of her Walkman, then skated to the opposite side of the rink to put her tape in the recorder.

"All right!" Behind her Haley's excited cheer rang out and seemed to echo throughout the huge rink.

13

Two days later Nikki was halfway out the door to her house when the phone rang. She grabbed the receiver and quickly said, "Hi!"

"Hi to you too!"

"Jill!" Nikki exclaimed.

"You sound like you're on your way somewhere," Jill said.

"You're right. Kathy held me over ten minutes on my lesson. My mother was late picking me up. And I have a dumb history paper due second period tomorrow," Nikki explained. "Dani is going to help me write it at the library. I'm already really late."

"Oh." Jill sounded disappointed. "I really was in the mood to talk—I got your note about Alex and Haley and Michael. Things sound really crazy at Silver Blades these days." Jill paused. "You all right?"

"No—yes—sort of," Nikki answered. "Oh, I really wish I could talk—"

"Not to worry!" Jill said. "Give me a call when you have more time. And thanks for that crazy stuffed animal. I love it! Hey, have you seen the new issue of *Rinkside?*"

"I just got the magazine in the mail today. It's in my book bag. I was going to look at it when I got to the library."

"Check it out. My coach, Holly Abbot, is interviewed in *Rinkside* this month and she even mentions *me!*"

"Wow!" Nikki checked her bag to be sure the magazine was still there. "I can't wait to read it. Miss you."

"Me too!" Jill replied, then they both hung up.

Half an hour later Nikki sat at a long oak table in the Seneca Hills Town Library waiting for inspiration to strike. Just two days, eleven hours, and ten minutes after the start of the Haley-Alex partnership, Nikki realized she had made the biggest mistake of her life. And there was nothing, *nothing* she could do about it.

Danielle was already scribbling her homework on a long yellow pad. She looked up. "Nikki," she whispered, "I told my mother to pick us up at seven-thirty. Have you even started writing your history paper yet?"

Nikki glanced guiltily at the stack of books and shrugged. "I can't do it now."

"It's now or never. It's due tomorrow." Danielle shook her head.

"I'm trying, Dani," she finally said. "But I can't seem to focus on anything."

"Wrong," diagnosed Danielle. "You're too focused— on Alex."

Nikki began to deny it, but she knew she couldn't fool Danielle. Besides, she was tired of trying to fool everyone, including herself. She tilted back in her chair and ran her tongue over her braces. "Okay, Dani, I give up. I admit it. I blew it. I never should have ended things with Alex."

"I know," Danielle said gently.

Nikki was surprised. "How?"

"It's pretty obvious, from the way you've been moping around the rink."

Nikki studied her hands. She had started biting her nails again. "It's weird. I know my singles program is getting stronger every day, but I really miss not being part of pairs. It feels so lonely, skating without Alex." Nikki's voice trembled. "I did a really good double flip today, and it felt strange that Alex wasn't there to see it."

"Hey, look who's here!"

Nikki looked up. Tori and Haley were over by the main desk, waving as they checked out some books. They detoured toward Nikki and Danielle.

"Oh, no, not Haley," Nikki groaned under her breath.

"Hey, I thought you two were friends," Danielle whispered.

Before Nikki could reply, Tori walked up. Nikki noticed Haley hang back. "Dani's got you doing homework?" Tori teased Nikki.

"Be careful, her brains might be catching," Haley joked.

Nikki hadn't been avoiding Haley at the rink, but she hadn't spent much time with her, either, since Alex had become Haley's partner.

There was an awkward silence. Then Haley noticed some guys from the Kent softball team walking out the door. "Look, I've got to go. Sorry, Tori. I'll call you later. I forgot I promised I'd check out their practice." She hurried away.

"Nikki, why aren't you talking to Haley?" charged Tori the minute Haley was out the door. Nikki opened her mouth, but no excuse would come out.

"Alex," volunteered Danielle. "She's upset that Haley is skating with Alex."

"That's not fair," Tori remarked. "You told Haley it was okay to skate with Alex. And now you're jealous?"

"I can't help it," Nikki moaned. "I thought I never wanted to skate with him again. Now . . . now maybe I think I was wrong. Maybe he didn't drop me on purpose. I saw the same thing happen to him and Haley on the ice the other day. His hand slipped. She fell hard. It wasn't his fault."

"So you want to skate pairs again?" Tori asked more gently.

Nikki traced a pattern on the table with her finger. She nodded. "I really miss it."

"Why don't you talk to Alex," Tori suggested. "Maybe you can get together again."

"No way!" Nikki shook her head. "I can't face him," she admitted. "I'm embarrassed about everything I've said to him. He probably hates me anyway."

Danielle chewed her lip, then brightened. "I've got it, Nikki. Just go to Kathy."

Nikki thought for a moment. "That's sneaky," she said finally. "I'd feel like I was going behind Haley's back. If Kathy finds her another partner, then I could speak up. But not now. I'm the one who changed my mind."

Nikki tilted her chair back, stretched out her legs, and stared out the window. "It's times like this I wish Jill were here. She'd think of something. She's always the creative—" Nikki sat bolt upright. "Jill!" she cried.

"Where?" Danielle practically fell off her chair.

"Not here, silly. But Jill called right before I left the house. I completely forgot about it. And Jill gave me the best idea!" Nikki cried.

"Shhh!" warned the librarian.

Nikki clapped her hand over her mouth. She motioned Danielle and Tori closer. "Jill called to tell me there's an interview with her coach in the latest issue of *Rinkside*."

Tori and Danielle exchanged puzzled glances.

"We could advertise in *Rinkside* for a partner," Nikki

explained, pulling the skating magazine out of her book bag.

"Awesome!" Danielle cried.

"Way to go, Nikki," Tori said. "You'll find a new partner, then Haley can stay—"

"No!" Nikki cried aloud, then cast a swift apologetic smile in the librarian's direction. She gathered her friends closer. "We don't find a partner for me. We find one for *Haley!*"

Dani's mouth formed a perfect O.

Tori gaped, then broke into a grin. "I *am* impressed. Nikki! I wish I had thought of it first!"

Nikki giggled. "Thinking about it is the easy part. Writing the ad is going to be hard."

"Not for me!" Danielle said proudly. "I love writing. All we need to do is figure out what makes a good partner for Haley."

"Red hair!" Tori and Nikki chorused. Nikki started to laugh, and once she started, she couldn't stop. She felt so relieved that she'd found an answer to her problem.

"That would be cute," Danielle said, "but we can't make the ad sound silly. We want people who are serious about competitive skating." She tore two sheets of paper off her pad and handed them to her friends. "Let's each make a list. What would make the perfect partner for Haley, skipping the hair part?"

Nikki quickly made her list, then handed it over to Danielle. She was barely able to sit still as Danielle studied their lists and drafted an ad.

"How's this sound?" Danielle said at last. She tucked her pencil behind her ear and read aloud.

"WANTED: Male Novice pairs partner who lives near Seneca Hills, PA. At least 5'7". I'm 5'2" and love to live dangerously . . . on the ice and off. Must have a good sense of humor and lots of competitive experience. Gymnastic background useful. Rush replies to Nikki Simon at 32 Oxford Drive, Seneca Hills, Pennsylvania."

"A sense of humor?" Tori wrinkled her nose. "What's that got to do with skating?

"Remember the bloody hand when she met Michael?" Danielle said.

"What if she pulls that again?" Nikki rolled her eyes. "I can picture it all now. We advertise. We find some perfect guy for Haley. Then that goofball blows it with some dumb joke." Nikki drummed her fingers on the table.

"What if Kathy doesn't go for this?" Danielle asked with a frown. "Or Haley?"

"Kathy will." Tori sounded definite. She dropped her voice to a whisper. "I heard Kathy tell Mr. Weiler that Alex and Haley are okay as a pairs team but don't have the same spark Haley and Michael did . . . or you and Alex. Alex is more lyrical and musical with a great sense of line, like Nikki. Haley needs a more energetic and athletic skater. If we found Haley a better partner, Kathy will go for it."

"And once Haley meets this super-energetic guy, she probably will too!" Danielle concluded.

"Right," Nikki said, feeling hopeful for the first time in days.

"We'll work it all out somehow. Let's hope someone answers this ad first," Danielle said.

"We'd better make sure the ad's in the next issue of *Rinkside*," Nikki said. "There's a competition in a couple of months. If Haley works with Alex much longer, Kathy might not let her change partners."

"Hey, think positive," Tori said. She thumbed through the magazine. "We don't have much time, but this is a great idea. It's going to work. And look, we're in luck. If we get this ad out tonight, we'll make the deadline for the next issue."

"How do we get it to them fast enough?" Nikki asked.

"Fax it. I'll use my mother's machine," Tori said. "She won't mind. She doesn't have to know what it's all about."

As Tori folded the paper and tucked it in her bag, Danielle suddenly exclaimed, "What if Haley sees it?"

"Why should she? Haley's not going to read the ads in the Personals," Tori said with confidence. "She has no idea she needs a new partner."

"Not yet!" gloated Nikki. "But she will, she will!"

14

"**C**an you believe all this stuff?" Tori exclaimed two weeks later. She shoved aside Nikki's old gray teddy bear and heaped a stack of résumés, photos, and envelopes on Nikki's bed. Then she plopped herself down on the blue-and-yellow quilt.

She and Danielle were sleeping over at Nikki's so that the three of them could go over all the replies they'd received since they'd placed the ad. Nikki felt almost giddy with excitement. She could barely sit still. She bounced across the room in her yellow pajamas to the rhythm of her favorite reggae CD.

The response to their ad in *Rinkside* was beyond her wildest dreams. "If you ever quit skating, you could work for an advertising company!" she told Danielle as she aimed a kernel of popcorn at her friend's mouth.

"Don't congratulate me yet!" Danielle warned, tilting her head back to catch the popcorn. She missed and cheerfully scooped it up with her fingers. "First let's see who wrote us and what they have to say about themselves." She sat cross-legged and piled some envelopes on her lap.

Nikki flopped facedown next to Tori and watched Danielle pull out the contents of the first envelope. A photo floated out.

"Hey," Dani said, "he looks like my father."

"Definitely too old," Tori said. She checked out his résumé. "He's ancient. He's twenty-seven years old."

"I should have put the age in the ad. I should have said male *teenage* skater," Danielle said. "Oh, wait, here's one!" Danielle scanned a letter. "He lives in Hawaii and has only been skating two months—total. But is into weight-lifting. Dig those biceps." She handed a photo to Nikki.

"No way!" Nikki decided, and reached for some popcorn. "Haley does not need a weight-lifter, thank you."

"Now, here's a real possibility!" Tori plunked a full-color glossy on the bed. The guy was cute and had one earring, like Haley. But his hair was cut into a Mohawk and dyed a million colors.

"Look at that hair!" Dani howled. "It looks like a rainbow."

"It matches his costume," Tori observed.

Nikki almost choked on her popcorn. "Now, he's just the type you want to bring home to meet the family," she cracked. She put the guy's photo and résumé in the reject pile.

"Hey, this one sounds good." Nikki read a résumé out loud. "He's skated pairs before. He won a silver in the Novice Regionals with his ex-partner."

"Cute too," said Tori, handing Danielle a black-and-white photo. "Let's put this in the serious-contenders pile."

"What's his name?" Nikki decided to start a list.

"Patrick McGuire."

"Funny," Nikki mused. "His name sort of sounds familiar." She picked up the glossy photo. "He's got a great smile, but I can't say I've seen him around before."

"He's from Mount Morris," Tori said, checking out the address on his letter. "That's not too far away. I feel like we should know him."

"Me too," Nikki added. "But I don't know why. Maybe we saw his name in some skating article. . . ."

"Okay, he's a keeper," Danielle declared. "Let's keep looking through this stuff and see if we can get three or four really strong guys."

"Then what?" asked Nikki, getting butterflies in her stomach. Suddenly finding even one person vaguely suitable for Haley made their plan seem all too real. Could she *really* pull it off? Would Kathy and Mr. Weiler go for it? What if Haley didn't want to give up Alex? Nikki squeezed her eyes shut and tried to push back that thought.

"Our next move is to call them up," Tori said.

"We need to set up an audition," Danielle said thoughtfully.

"But when? And what about Kathy and Mr. Weiler?" Nikki asked.

Tori's blue eyes sparkled. "I figured all that out already." She paused for effect, then went on. "Next Sunday morning Mr. Weiler and Kathy are going off to judge a competition down in Bristol. We'll schedule tryouts then. They'll be at least fifty miles away from the arena when we hold our auditions."

"It *is* a public skating day," Danielle reminded her, looking worried.

Tori shrugged. "No problem. Haven't you noticed? Now that it's the end of May, not many people are spending Sundays inside at the rink. It's been pretty empty the last couple of weeks—I've been getting in extra practice Sunday mornings."

"That's right," Nikki remembered. "I had a special session with Kathy a few weeks ago on a Sunday. We practically had the ice to ourselves."

"But won't the guys think something's weird when the coaches aren't at the rink?" Nikki asked a moment later.

"We'll have to make up some story," Danielle said.

"And what about Haley? How do we get her to skate with these guys?" Nikki asked.

"Haley?" Tori and Danielle cried in unison.

"She doesn't get it. . . ." Tori said to Danielle.

Danielle looked at Nikki with great pity.

"Haley isn't going to audition these guys. You are!"

"Me?" Nikki cried. "Hey, wait a minute, we can't trick these people into coming here and trying out and letting them think they're skating with me when they're going to be skating with Haley and—"

Danielle cut her off. "Trust me," she said. "This is going to work. But *not* if we get Haley in on it too soon. It's the coaches who aren't thrilled with their partnership, not Haley. Haley's pretty friendly with Alex—she doesn't even *know* she wants to dump him for another guy."

"You're the pairs expert of this crowd," Tori said to Nikki. "Dani and I can't skate with the guys. We're both rotten at pairs. It's up to you to find the perfect guy for Haley. We'll introduce her to Mr. Right later."

"And when it comes to Haley, have I got a plan. . . ." Tori chuckled and motioned the other girls closer.

15

"**H**ere goes nothing," Nikki murmured the morning of the tryouts. She was wearing her best skating dress and had even borrowed Tori's pearl stud earrings for the occasion. "I didn't feel this nervous when I tried out for Silver Blades!" she confided in Tori as they left the girls' locker room.

The rink was having a public session, but as Tori predicted, the crowd was thin. It would make testing Haley's possible partners easier.

Halfway to the rink Nikki made an about-face. "I can't do this," she said. Her knees had turned to rubber. "This is a crazy idea. What were we thinking?"

"You can't freak out now." Tori gripped her arm and steered her firmly down the hall. "Remember the plan. I told Haley I wanted her to come over later to help me on my layback spin. Believe me, getting Haley to give up Sunday softball wasn't easy."

Danielle was dressed in her dark leggings, and a black oversized sweater she had borrowed from her mother. With her hair up in a French twist she looked a lot older, maybe even sixteen, Nikki thought.

Danielle clutched a clipboard to her chest, trying to look official. She hovered nervously just outside the boys' locker room. She winked at Nikki as Nikki and Tori ducked into the rink. Danielle was supposed to corral the would-be partners as they came into the building, *before* they had a chance to ask one of the administration or maintenance people where to sign up for pairs tryouts. Nikki was pretty impressed by Danielle. She looked awfully efficient and extremely organized. The clipboard of course came from Tori's mom's desk. Nikki only hoped the boys would be so nervous, they wouldn't notice the bright pink Carsen Design Group logo emblazoned on top.

Nikki and Tori stationed themselves right inside the rink door. "She's coming, she's coming!" Tori cried frantically, then reached out and tucked back a stray hair into Nikki's ponytail. "Be cool!" she warned.

Danielle opened the door. "What's the matter?" Tori whispered to Danielle. "You look like you swallowed a lemon!"

"This is *not* going to work," Danielle murmured, rolling her eyes. She flashed Nikki a pitying look, then held the door open wide and beckoned a very tall boy inside. Danielle then broke into a very wide, very fake smile. Nikki drew in a quick breath.

"Definitely no competition for Alex," Tori whispered. She squeezed Nikki's arm, then marched up to the boy, her hand outstretched.

"Welcome to Silver Blades," Tori said in her best Kent Academy prep-school accent. "You must be . . ."

"I—I'm Blade." Blade was about six foot one and all bones. He was lanky, loose-limbed, and awkward. He looked shyer than Kyle, like he planned to bolt any second.

Nikki remembered now. They had picked Blade because he had a cool name. He hadn't sent a picture. He had studied with a couple of good coaches, though.

"This is Nikki. She's going to skate with you." Tori's eyes practically lasered Nikki, daring her to back out now.

Nikki managed a very weak smile. "Yes. Uh—I am. Are you warmed up yet?"

"A little." He blushed and didn't quite meet her eyes. "I was here early—about an hour ago. No one seemed to know about the tryouts." He cast a nervous glance around the rink.

Nikki darted a quick glance at Tori. Tori looked at Danielle. Danielle looked back at Tori.

Tori waved vaguely in the air. "Umm, yes. We've narrowed down the selection to just a few boys—"

"Already?" Blade looked confused.

Tori ignored him and went on. "So we didn't think we needed to inform the *entire* rink staff. . . ."

Danielle made a big thing of checking her watch.

"We're running behind schedule. Nikki, you'd better start the tryout now."

"Are the coaches here?" Blade asked, following Nikki onto the ice. He handed Nikki his résumé. She stared at it, then cast a helpless look at Tori.

Tori marched up to the barrier and reached her hand out and took the sheet of paper.

"Blade wants to know about the coaches," Nikki said, but Tori was already marching back toward Danielle. They were both giggling. Nikki wanted to strangle them. Instead she forced herself to smile at Blade and say in her most professional-sounding voice, "The coaches aren't here today. What I mean is," she added as they began skating around the rink, "we're the pre-audition committee. We make the first cut. If the tryout goes well today, we'll schedule an appointment with the coach . . . uh . . . coaches." She hoped she sounded convincing. As they warmed up, she noticed Blade was a good skater, just much too tall for Haley.

"So let's try a side-by-side sit spin," she told him when they'd circled the rink a few times.

"Right."

They went into the spin. Nikki whirled to the right. Blade to the left. When Nikki came out of her spin, she couldn't find Blade. He was still spinning, several feet away, with his arms low over his leg.

"Uh, that's enough, Blade," she shouted over the noise of the rink.

"Oh," he said, coming out of the turn. "You don't

want to see something else?" He looked so hopeful, Nikki felt terrible. She searched her mind, wondering if having him go through a couple of more moves was kinder than letting him just go back to the changing room now.

Danielle cleared her throat loudly and pointed at the rink clock.

"No, Blade. Sorry. We've got someone else scheduled, but thanks."

Nikki shook his hand and waited until he had left for the locker room before gliding up to Danielle.

"Bad news!" Danielle said.

"Whose idea was this anyway?" Nikki joked, and Danielle laughed.

The second skater turned out to be inexperienced. And by the time Nikki skated with the third candidate, she had almost given up hope. Darrell Markham had slimy hands. The fourth skater, Kevin Rodriguez, couldn't manage even a double axel.

"Is that it?" Nikki asked Danielle after the last skater left the rink.

"Excuse me, is Nikki Simon here?" a friendly voice asked. "I think she may be a coach."

Nikki winced, then turned around. She gaped at the boy standing in front of them. He was about five foot seven with warm brown eyes and red hair. He could be Haley's brother, was Nikki's first thought.

"*You* must be Patrick!" Danielle beamed. The skater looked about fifteen and wore a green cotton turtleneck underneath a black body suit.

Nikki couldn't take her eyes off Patrick's red hair. Even Tori was speechless.

"I'm Danielle Panati," Danielle introduced herself. "This is Tori Carsen and this is Nikki—"

"Simon," Nikki interjected. She offered Patrick her hand. "I'm not a coach, though. I'm a pairs skater."

"You're the one looking for a partner?" he asked. "Don't I know your name from somewhere?"

Nikki gulped. "I don't think so. I haven't been skating pairs long, and my partner and I . . . uh, just broke up," Nikki floundered. How could she possibly explain this complicated situation?

"It's hard losing a partner," Patrick commiserated.

"Right!" said Nikki with great relief.

As Patrick handed over his résumé to Danielle, Tori suddenly cried out, "Oh, no! Look over there, Dani." She pointed through the rink door to the lobby.

"It's Mr. Weiler!" Nikki exclaimed. "He must have gotten back from the competition earlier!"

"What's wrong?" Patrick asked.

"Nothing to worry about," Danielle said coolly, motioning to Tori to do something—fast! "Patrick, why don't you try out with Nikki now?"

Nikki led him onto the ice as Tori opened the lobby door and called out, "Mr. Weiler, I need to talk to you in your office *now!*"

"So why are you looking for a partner?" Nikki asked as they warmed up. She couldn't believe what a close call they just had with Mr. Weiler.

Patrick's smile dimmed. "My last partner, Karen

Carns, was hurt in a car accident about six months ago. She's okay now, but she can't skate again. I'm still training for singles . . . but once you're used to a partner, it's weird skating alone."

Don't I know it! thought Nikki.

He went on to explain that he lived twenty miles away. "I'm a freshman in high school over in Mount Morris, but I can arrange my schedule to train here."

"Good," said Nikki. She tried not to get too excited—so far Patrick seemed perfect for Haley, but she still hadn't seen him skate.

When Patrick said he was ready, she suggested that they try the sit spin. Then they did a flying camel and several lifts. With every move Nikki's hopes rose. He was perfect—just perfect.

"That's enough, I think," she said finally. "You're really great, Patrick."

"So when do we start?" he asked. He skated back and forth in front of her, his hands on his hips. He looked happy and pleased. "And when do I meet the coaches?"

"Uh," Nikki fumbled, looking over toward Danielle and Tori. Maybe the two of them could help her to explain this to Patrick.

Standing in the front row of seats was Haley. She was with Alex. Both of them were staring in Nikki's direction.

Even from where Nikki stood, in the center of the rink, she could see that Haley's eyes were huge with surprise.

Patrick followed her gaze and seemed to notice Haley.

Abruptly Nikki took his hand and pulled him toward one end of the rink. Sure now that Haley was there and watching, Nikki wanted to show him off.

"Is something wrong?" he asked, yanking down the sleeve of his shirt.

Nikki shook her head. "Let's try just one more move. Your choice," she said.

"How's your death spiral?"

Nikki froze. She hadn't done a death spiral since Alex had dropped her, and she had to admit that the pairs move still terrified her. She also knew that if she ever wanted to skate pairs again, with Alex or anyone else, she'd have to execute this movement— and execute it without fear.

She nodded to Patrick, then grit her teeth and took his hand. His grip was firm as she went into the spin and lay back horizontally only inches above the surface of the ice. A moment later she completed the death spiral. She had done it! She felt triumphant, and confident, and exhilarated. She turned to Patrick. "I'm sure when the coaches get here and you go through a more formal tryout, you'll be more than welcome to train as a pairs skater here," Nikki told him. She skated over to the barrier, making sure they landed right near Haley and Alex.

"Oh, Haley!" Nikki said sweetly. "Nice to see you guys." She swallowed hard and even smiled at Alex.

He gave her a confused stare. Nikki moistened her lips, and said. "I don't believe you've met—"

"*Patrick*—what are you doing here?" Haley's shriek echoed through the rink.

"Haley? Haley Arthur?"

Patrick gaped at Haley. Haley gaped at Patrick. Where had Haley and Patrick met before? Nikki wondered.

"Where's Michael?" Patrick looked around, right past Alex. "I haven't seen you guys since you took that gold at the competition last winter."

"Gone," Haley said, leaning over the barrier. "Would you believe it, he moved to Japan?"

"I lost my partner too," Patrick said softly, and told his story.

Nikki stood there looking from Patrick to Haley. She tried not to look directly at Alex. She could sense that he was totally baffled by Patrick and the pairs performance he'd just witnessed.

"But why are you here?" Haley finally asked Patrick again.

"I came to try out to see if I could work with Nikki," he said. "I saw her ad and—"

"You're skating pairs again, Nikki?" Alex interrupted.

At that Nikki looked him right in the eye. "I miss it."

"Oh." For a moment he looked down at the floor.

Patrick continued to stare at Haley. "I wish I had known . . . about Michael and you," he murmured.

Tori playfully punched Nikki's arm. "Tell them, Nikki."

"Tell them what?" Haley asked.

Nikki decided the time had come to tell the truth. "Patrick," she said, turning to him. "One thing about this tryout. It wasn't to skate with me."

He frowned. Haley squinted. Alex looked more confused than ever.

Quickly Nikki went on. "Actually, Patrick, we didn't know Haley knew you. We just wanted to find her a new partner." Nikki looked right at Alex as she said that.

Haley's face was impossible to read. "Is this some kind of joke?" she asked. "Are you trying to get back at me for the spider or—"

"No!" Danielle, Tori, and Nikki shouted all at once.

"It isn't a joke," Nikki continued. "We just thought you didn't skate with Alex as well as you skated with Michael. Alex isn't really your type, Haley."

"Admit it." Tori playfully punched Haley's arm and put one arm around Alex. "You two are not made for each other. Haley, you need someone who's into funkier music and is less romantic!"

Haley began to grin.

Then Danielle went on to explain the whole scheme. "See, it was all Nikki's idea . . ." she began. By the end everyone but Alex was laughing. Nikki was so relieved that Haley seemed to be really into the whole idea.

"So do you want to see how *we* skate together?"

Patrick asked Haley. "I've been dying to skate with you for ages."

"You bet!" she said, and flashed Nikki the warmest smile. "Thanks."

Nikki and Haley exchanged a huge hug, then Haley and Patrick took to the ice. Nikki turned around to talk to Alex, but he was gone.

16

"Alex?" Nikki cried. She couldn't believe it. He was upset about losing Haley. Nikki hadn't even thought about that part of her plan. She had been so caught up in making sure that *Haley* wasn't angry that she hadn't had time to explain things to Alex. He probably thought that she was trying to sabotage his partnership with Haley or something.

Nikki put on her skate guards and raced into the lobby. Alex was heading for the snack bar. His head was down and his hands were shoved into his pockets.

Nikki finally caught up to him right outside the pro shop. "Alex."

He stopped in his tracks and didn't turn around. His shoulders looked tight and tense. Nikki hesitated. She wasn't sure what to say.

"Alex, let me explain."

Alex turned and gave an exaggerated shrug. "What's to explain?"

"Patrick, for one thing . . ." Nikki paused, and stared at the beige lobby carpet. "Us . . ."

"What's that supposed to mean?"

"Alex, I'm sorry. I'm really really sorry. . . ." Nikki started, then her voice trailed off. She took a deep breath. "I want to skate with you again. I miss you. I miss *skating* with you."

Alex took a long time before he answered. "I miss you too."

"Does that mean you want to skate together?" Nikki asked hopefully.

"Even though I dropped you on purpose?" Alex blurted.

Nikki felt about two inches high. "I'm sorry. I realize now that wasn't true. You didn't drop me on purpose. I just figured you were so mad at me . . . after that picnic."

"I am. I was." Alex tugged at his hair. "I'm not even sure what we were fighting about anymore."

Nikki paused. "We were fighting about Kyle."

"Right, I made you lie to him." Alex turned stony again.

"No. I'm sorry for that too. I lied to him. That was stupid and dumb and that was all my fault, but . . ."

"But . . ." Alex threw his hands up. "But what?"

"But I thought you wanted me to be your girlfriend," Nikki blurted out.

Alex looked at her like she had grown three heads.

"Don't look at me like that." Nikki squirmed a little. "What did you expect me to think . . . after the balloons, the way you kept putting your arm around me at the ballet."

Alex had the strangest expression on his face. He seemed to be trying not to laugh. "You're really serious. You thought I wanted to *date* you?"

"What was I supposed to think?" Nikki's voice grew shrill.

"That I just wanted to be friends. Pairs partners should spend time together, get to know each other. I read a whole article on that in *Rinkside* magazine. To build trust, you have to learn to communicate. Without trust between us . . ." He raked his hands through his hair and looked confused. "I thought sending balloons was a pretty cool thing to do.

"Nikki, don't take this the wrong way," Alex went on, "but . . . I never even dreamed of you being my girlfriend."

"You didn't?" Nikki blushed a little. "Uh—because of Kyle?"

"Because I've got a girlfriend."

"You do?" Nikki felt her eyes go wide. "But Tori never mentioned that . . . or Haley . . . or—"

"Tori doesn't know her. She doesn't go to Kent. She goes to Hawley. She's an eighth-grader like me."

Hawley? It was a private school in Montville. Nikki suddenly felt so absolutely embarrassed, she wanted to die. She covered her face with her hands and groaned.

Alex tapped on her hands with his fist. "Hey, anyone home?" He pried her fingers off her face. "Not that you wouldn't make a very nice girlfriend," he said. He faked a gallant bow and took her hand.

Nikki pulled her hand away from him. Okay, so I misinterpreted Alex's behavior, she told herself. But I had good reasons for thinking he was interested in me as a girlfriend. Even my friends thought he liked me that way—at least Dani did.

Nikki folded her arms in front of her chest. "What was I supposed to think when you put your arm around me at the ballet?" she asked him. "And when you didn't tell your father that I wasn't your girlfriend?"

"I just hate to explain personal stuff to my dad," Alex said. "He'd want to know everything, and I just didn't want to get into it."

Nikki could understand that. Sometimes parents asked too many questions. "Then why did you let Kyle think we were going out together?" she persisted.

Alex shifted from foot to foot and grinned sheepishly as he admitted, "I guess I was sort of enjoying it. I thought that it was kind of neat that Kyle was jealous of me."

"Alex! I can't believe you would do that to me!" Nikki said. "How am I supposed to trust you when you almost ruined everything with Kyle and me?"

Alex for once was speechless. He hung his head, and Nikki went on.

"Skating partners have got to be straight with each other, Alex. Okay?"

Alex took a big breath, looked into Nikki's eyes, and said, "I'm sorry, Nikki. I really blew it. Big-time."

Nikki stared back at him, trying to read his expression.

"You've got to believe me, Nikki. I'm really sorry. Let's call a truce and be friends." Alex gave her a big smile.

Nikki smiled back. He means it, she thought.

Just then Kyle brushed past them and entered the pro shop.

Nikki's smile collapsed.

"He's still upset?" asked Alex.

"I guess," Nikki said. "I haven't spoken with him since the picnic. Look, I don't feel like talking about this anymore, okay? Can we talk later?"

"No!" Alex said firmly.

A few seconds later Kyle blew out of the pro shop, pocketing some laces.

"Dorset, wait up," Alex said. He grabbed the back of Kyle's hockey jersey.

"Kyle, there's been a big mistake."

"I don't want to hear this." Kyle jerked away from Alex and refused to meet Nikki's eyes.

"Yes, you do. I am not dating Nikki. I never was. I have a girlfriend and I should have said that at the picnic."

Nikki was impressed that Alex was being honest with Kyle.

Kyle finally looked at Nikki. "Then why did you lie to me?"

"It's a long story," she said slowly.

"You two have to work this out." Alex pushed them together. "Dorset, she's great, but she's really just my skating partner."

"I am?" Nikki said, suddenly realizing that she and Alex really were partners again.

"We'll talk later. Figure out what to tell Kathy." Alex waved good-bye and went back toward the rink.

Kyle cleared his throat. "What's going on, Nikki?"

"I lied to you and I'm sorry, but you were so jealous of Alex."

Kyle didn't deny it. "What was I supposed to think? Balloons, trips to the ballet . . . hugging you all the time." Kyle propped his chin on his hockey stick and just looked at Nikki. "You spend so much time with him."

"Pairs partners have to. We have to practice so much. You know that." Nikki felt a little frustrated that he didn't understand that, but she also understood how Kyle could feel jealous of Alex. "Alex *does* go a little overboard at times," Nikki admitted.

Kyle chewed his lip. "That's for sure," he said in the direction of his shoes. Then he glanced up, and Nikki looked into his eyes.

"I'll never lie to you again," Nikki said softly.

Kyle smiled and nodded. "Okay," he said. "Want to go to the soccer game this afternoon?"

"I'd love it," Nikki answered eagerly.

Kyle stood hugging his hockey stick and rocked back and forth on his skates as he grinned. Then he plunked on his helmet and turned on his heels and loped toward the hockey rink.

In the dressing room later Haley and Nikki sat across from each other, smiling.

"Can you believe it? We found you a partner with red hair!" Nikki said.

"Can *you* believe it," Haley said. "I'm just as glad to be rid of Alex. He's too serious and romantic for me!"

Nikki balled up a sock and tossed it at Haley.

Haley stuck her tongue out at Nikki. Then her face softened into a silly smile. "You have no idea what you just did out there . . . pairing me up with Patrick. I love Patrick. I've always wanted to skate with Patrick, but he and Karen were a really tight team. I really, really like him, Nikki."

"But why didn't Kathy put you two in touch?" Nikki wondered half to herself.

Haley rolled her big eyes. "Because of me, stupid . . . and you. She thought I wanted to skate with Alex. Plus Patrick didn't know for sure until about two weeks ago that Karen was finished with skating for good."

Both girls fell silent a moment. The thought of any kind of injury putting an end to skating was too awful to contemplate.

Haley shook her head, as if to shake off that thought. "Anyway it all worked out for the best." She giggled, and confided in a whisper, "Patrick said he always wanted to skate with me too . . . but when Michael and I took that gold, he figured it would never happen."

"Wrong!" Nikki laughed.

When Danielle and Tori walked in a moment later, Haley winked at Nikki.

"Sit here, Dani." Haley patted the seat next to her.

"What's up, guys?" Danielle said, and obediently plopped down next to Haley. From underneath her was a loud, flat sound. Haley cracked up, and Nikki started to giggle. Danielle jumped up and shrieked. "Haley Arthur, one more joke and you're . . ."

"History?" Nikki suggested, handing Haley her whoo-pee cushion.

Nikki burst through the front door that evening. Her father's car was gone, but her mother was in the kitchen.

"Mom," she tossed down her duffel and pirouetted on the slick kitchen floor. "I'm back with Alex again," she announced, "And I'm also back with Kyle. We had a great time at the soccer game today." She threw her arms around her mother and gave her a good long hug.

Her mother hugged her back and then held her at arm's length. She looked completely confused. "Kyle? I never knew you two weren't together."

Nikki grinned at her. "I know. I never got to tell you about it. You and Dad have been so worried or something lately."

Nikki's mother took a deep breath. "Nikki, I'm sorry. I've been a bit preoccupied lately. You've had a lot going on, and I haven't been there for you. . . ."

"It's okay, Mom," Nikki said. The truth was, it *was* okay now. She *had* missed her mom and had really needed a shoulder to cry on. But she had managed pretty well on her own.

"Nikki, I've got some pretty big news. It affects all of us . . . including you." Mrs. Simon sounded so serious, Nikki got scared.

Nikki held her breath. Don't tell me we're going to move. She prayed silently. Don't tell me you've got a business opportunity somewhere else. Don't say Dad got a great job in Texas.

"Sweetie, don't look so upset. It's nothing bad," Nikki's mother said. She toyed with the salt shaker and took a deep breath, then announced, "I'm pregnant. You're going to have a brother . . . or sister."

"You're having a baby?" Nikki couldn't believe she'd heard right.

"Your dad and I are so happy. We've known for a while. But the doctor suggested that I wait a few more weeks before I told anyone." She looked at Nikki with glowing eyes. "But I just had to tell you."

Nikki hugged her mother hard.

"Please don't tell your friends yet," Mrs. Simon cautioned. "It's still a little early."

Nikki promised. Her mind was racing with so many thoughts. The idea of suddenly having a brother or a sister . . . She wasn't sure how she really felt about that. It had been just her at home for so long.

But at least, she told herself, she knew she had a date to go to the movies with Kyle next Friday. And she had definitely made a new, funny friend in Haley Arthur. And with Alex as her partner again, Nikki was sure her skating would be better than ever. Suddenly a gold medal in pairs didn't seem that far away.

Today everything was great. She'd think about the new baby tomorrow.